PAWS ON THE PIER

M.G. WETHERHOLT

ONE

BEING travel-sized is not always advantageous.

By the third time Olivia's mascara missile hit me in the back, I wondered if this trip wasn't better as a dream than as reality. The nice thing about being a mouse is that you can fit in very small spaces without being seen. The sucky thing about being a mouse is that you can be easily squished by practically everything.

I thought of my father, who tried to warn me off this trip. "Hazel Huntington Graymouse," he squeaked. "What if you can't sneak into the luggage home? What if the luggage lands on you? What if the beach house has a big cat, or a small dog, or an exterminator?"

He always used my full name when he was worried, and I missed his loving concern, but it had been so long since I'd seen the ocean. I loved our previous life on the beach. If it wasn't for what had happened at the pier, our family would still be together and living there.

I should probably explain—when my siblings and I were born, there was a particularly unusual lightning storm that night, which hit the pier and ran down the wiring to our nest. Our mother died but we survived. The next morning, we found we could understand human language. Then later, when my brother got caught in a net by a child, he yelled out, "Let me go!"

That's how we found out we could speak human as well. As surprising as it was to us, it was quite a shock to the little two-legged beast.

Until last week, I had not paid much attention to Olivia Bent, the girl who took up space in what was supposed to be my room. She is vain, shallow, and mean. She is also the least likely person I would ever talk to, even if I did want to talk to humans.

I don't see a need to speak with two-legged giants who want to kill me at every opportunity, so I have kept my words to myself. And I definitely don't want to talk to Olivia. My biggest enjoyment is to jump out at her from behind her mirror and send her squealing from the room.

But I heard her whine and mope and complain

about *needing* a trip to the beach house with her besties. When "Mums and Daddy" said yes, I made my plans. Now here I was in a Caboodle, bouncing around the trunk of her Audi.

After a lifetime of road noise and faint laughter from the girls, I finally felt the car jerk to a stop and heard the engine stop engine-ing. Car doors slammed, more laughter, and then silence. I hoped they wouldn't leave the luggage out here all day— this trunk was already hot enough without sitting in bright beach sunlight.

A popping sound and a few musical notes announced a beam of light in the seam of the makeup kit. As the trunk opened, I heard the end of Olivia's condescending orders.

"…and don't just throw them in the rooms, Leo. Take care with our bags."

She must have gone, because I heard several choice words from Leo, spoken low enough to keep him out of trouble. I'd repeat them, but I think I'm still too young. In addition to the colorful opinion he expressed about Olivia's orders, he also mumbled succinct yet graphic descriptions of what he'd rather do with Olivia or any one of her friends.

Again, I'll leave that to the imagination.

I felt my container lifting, followed by the rough bouncing of being carried quickly and carelessly.

Doors were slammed open and slammed shut, and then I heard the thud of items being thrown. Luggage. Was he going to throw my hiding place? How far?

I braced myself for a tumble, just as everything flipped upside down, hit the ground, and slid. Jars and bottles hurtled toward me, and I pushed at them with all four paws to keep them from running into me. One of the jars lost its lid and powder exploded into the space.

I wasn't going to be squished, I was going to be suffocated by eye shadow.

"Leo!" Olivia screamed. "What the even?!?"

"Sorry, miss. It slipped."

"Slipped my eye," I mumbled.

"What was that?" Olivia picked up the makeup caboodle. "Did you hear something?"

"I didn't hear nuthin'," Leo said.

I smiled and, lowering my voice, muttered, "I just wanna hear you cry for more."

"What did you say?" Olivia snapped.

"I didn't say nuthin'," Leo said.

This could be a fun game. "We could have a good time," I growled softly.

That's when I heard a slap.

"Get. OUT." I could feel her anger shaking the

makeup kit still in her arms. "I'm calling Daddy RIGHT NOW to FIRE YOU!"

"Good luck with that." Leo's voice was getting further away.

Olivia set the makeup kit down and opened it. I scrunched myself into a corner.

"Ohmahgawd, what a mess." Her fingers reached in, picking up the jars and bottles. "My Dior shadow —I just bought that."

Fingertips came toward me, and I squeezed myself flatter against the side of the case. Olivia touched the edge of the opened jar, pulling her hand back when she encountered the powder.

"Ugh, I need a tissue, this is going to get all over my nails."

She turned to the nightstand and opened a drawer. This gave me enough time to leap out of the kit and race across the room. I slid under a door and found myself in the bathroom. There was a small open window near the mirror, so I scampered up the exposed plumbing and made my escape, stopping briefly to look at my reflection. I was very purple and sparkly.

Crawling along the roofline, I reached the beachfront and stopped to sit in one of the gables and look at the scene. The coastline ran southwest, and the early afternoon sun was sitting high, giving the waves a disco-ball glimmer. Tide was low but the waves were not, lifting into curls and crashing to the sand before being pulled back out to sea. The rush of water and wind, out and in like my breath, tempted to lull me into napping. Not a bad idea, but first, I needed to feel sand between my twenty toes.

I made my way down the woodwork, from the doorframe to the window, and finally to the deck, where I shot off to the beach. The sand was deliciously warm and soft. I found a decent-sized footprint to drop down and roll in, splashing the sand up and over myself, giving my gray fur a shake before rolling again and again. It was a luxurious way to remove the eye powder. Finally de-glittered, I trotted to where the water met the land and stood until I felt the very tip of the wave wash ashore. I wished I could go further, but when you are very small, the least amount of water can whoosh you away.

If there's a next life, I thought, *maybe I should return as something bigger.*

TWO

IT DIDN'T TAKE LONG for me to grow hungry. I looked down the shore. There were plenty of houses and even some restaurants to eat from. I glanced back at Olivia's beach house and considered my options. Restaurants were smorgasbords of delight, but they were also usually on the lookout for what they called "vermin." I shuddered as I mouthed the word.

The beach house was a familiar place—it was where I grew up. I knew the kitchen, and more importantly, knew there were no traps to snap me in half. Sighing, I turned and trotted back. Besides, I had promised my family that this was just a vacation. I knew if I spent much time in the town, I might not return.

I was in the pantry, chewing a hole in a bag of peanuts, when I heard the girls' voices. I peeked through a slit in the doorframe.

"OMG, Olivia, that Leo guy is a creeper," Brina said. She was short and slender with long, straight black hair. All the other girls thought she was beautiful.

She wasn't as pretty as a mouse, so I'm no judge.

"Ugh," Olivia said. "I told Daddy to fire him last year, but Daddy said something about knowing him in college and he needs a job, blah-blah-blah."

"Did he break any of your stuff?" Ashley asked. She was the baby of the group, a twenty-one year-old blonde who described herself as fluffy.

"My special edition Dior shadow and my Fenti powder, both opened and spilled everywhere," Olivia said. "You?"

"My Niacinamide serum," Claire said, running her hand through her burgundy highlights. "Everything is drenched and now I'm down to just my Vitamin C."

"Well, that does it," Olivia told them. "Maybe Daddy doesn't care when Leo messes with our family, but not our guests." She pulled her phone from her pocket and pressed some buttons.

These humans, and the peanuts, were beginning

to bore me, so I moved further down the shelf, where I found snack-sized packages of chocolate-iced donuts. They were hidden behind a canister of flour, so I assumed they were guilty pleasures.

I helped myself to a package.

When I could not stuff one more yeasty morsel into my mouth, I went back to Olivia's room. I wanted to find the crevice in the wall that my family had lived in before the big move. We hadn't planned to move at all that winter, but when the homeowners packed up, my youngest brother got trapped in one of the suitcases and in trying to free him, we all ended up hitching a ride to Riverside, a desert of no redemption.

Now I searched my old home, hoping no other mouse family had moved in. I wouldn't begrudge another family from finding shelter, but I found my special gift for human speech had rendered other mice boring. Even when I immersed myself in mouse-speak, I was aware of my difference and felt like the odd mouse out.

I remembered the corner and was scurrying along the wall when I heard Olivia's familiar shriek. I looked up but she wasn't staring at me, she was looking to the right, pointing dramatically. I followed her hand and saw another mouse, running along the baseboard like me. Only he wasn't like me, he was white with pink eyes. For a moment, I stopped and stared. Olivia's feet shook the floor as she ran out of the room.

"I can't sleep in there, it has mice!" she wailed.

Shaking myself out of my stupor, I ran after the white mouse. He disappeared into the crevice—my family's old home. I slipped in after him and stopped to introduce myself. He glared at me, his pink eyes glowing, before slipping into the drywall and running away.

I chased after him, scampering through the dark corridors until I cornered him against a wooden beam. He scrambled up the wood, so I followed.

"Squeak!" I called out to make him stop. "Squeak-squeakers-squee!"

That made him run faster. I watched as he reached the top of the wall and disappeared. Climbing after him, I launched myself over the beam and saw daylight—we had reached the eaves of the roof.

The white mouse perched on a section of framing, gazing down with a stricken expression in his pink eyes. I looked down and saw Olivia and her friends, coming out on the porch with drinks and snacks.

While jumping into the middle of their fun sounded like a good game, I decided to pause and listen to them nattering about their lives. It was always nice to know things about humans, things I could use later.

"Can you believe it?" Olivia asked. "Daddy said he's not going to fire Leo."

"How rude!" Ashley reached for a pita chip. "I can't believe he'd choose that creep over you."

"He said he'd have a 'talk' with him." Olivia poured more drink from a pitcher into her glass. I didn't know what kind of drink it was, except it was green and smelled like it would burn my throat.

"A talk. Pfft," Brina scoffed. "Like my mom used to have with me. 'Brina, dear, we mustn't be rude to our guests.' As if that made me more polite."

"What I want to know," Claire leaned forward, "is what the caretaker has on your dad."

Olivia paused her drinking. "What do you mean?"

Her friend tucked a strand of burgundy hair behind one ear, then gestured. "Anyone could take care of this place. Your dad could replace Leo tomorrow—probably sooner than that. I know he told you he and Leo are pals from college, but I can think of another reason he wouldn't fire him—Leo knows a secret and won't tell as long as he's paid off."

Even from my perch under the roof, I could see Olivia frowning.

"I'll take it up with Mums," Olivia said, shaking her head. "In the meantime, we've been invited to a party at the pier. I told them we'd bring a pitcher of margaritas and a bag of chips."

"What time?" Brina asked. "I gotta do my hair."

"Do what with it?" Ashley took another sip of her drink. "Make it sleeker and shinier? It's already gorgeous."

"Aw, Ash, you're sweet," Brina said. "It just feels a little flat on my head. I'd like to foof it out a bit."

Olivia looked at her watch. "I said we'd be over in an hour, so let's all go foof something and meet in the kitchen by seven. I'll mix up another pitcher."

They strolled inside the house, and I sat back against the eave. Where did that white mouse go? I crawled toward the last place I'd seen him, but he was gone. Following the roofing beams inward, I came upon a small attic, barely as large as the one bathroom in the three-bedroom bungalow.

The last time I'd been in this space, it was full of dust and cobwebs and boxes of people stuff—photos and papers and doodads. Now I barely recognized it. Curiosity overwhelmed my caution, and I snuck down the beam to have a look around. There was an old, bare mattress on the floor, covered with a frayed blanket. The only other thing that would count as furnishings was a television on the opposite wall.

Several plastic grocery bags were scattered on the floor, requiring investigation. They were all filled with fast food wrappers. I found an empty burger wrapper and nibbled on the cheese that had melted to the paper. I was looking for more scraps when I heard heavy footsteps and the scrape of flooring being pushed aside.

Quickly scampering out of sight, I saw a square of floor shifting, allowing someone to heft himself through the hole. It was Leo, who had apparently created his own mancave by cutting a hole in the ceiling over the garage. He crawled over to the mattress, dragging a paper bag. Reaching under the blanket, he pulled out a remote control and held it toward the TV. One click and the monitor lit up.

I had just begun to feel bad about getting Leo in trouble with Olivia. He wasn't the nicest of men and was no doubt thinking what I muttered. But at least he had the smarts to keep his mouth shut.

"Just in time for the floor show," he said, and dug into his paper bag, pulling out a bottle and popping the top.

I looked at the TV that had his attention and my

whiskers stiffened. The screen was split into four sections, each section displaying one of the three bedrooms and the last section showing the bathroom interior. Leo had planted cameras to spy on the occupants.

THREE

OLIVIA WASN'T my favorite person, if I could have such a thing, but she didn't deserve this. Studying the TV, I determined where the cameras had to be located. The girls were changing their clothes, so I needed to be quick. I decided on the bathroom camera first—Claire was preparing to get into the shower.

Scampering down a space in the flooring, I raced down the wall toward the room, feeling about and sniffing for wires. I'd chewed through quite a few in my time. Rubber has a delicate taste, compared to its strong aroma. I found the camera easily, taped against the drywall with duct tape, another favorite thing for me to chew.

It was easy to tear the tape with my incisors, sending the camera to hang down the inner wall, now recording blackness. I figured I'd dislodge the cameras first, then chew the wires at my leisure.

I was on my way to the first bedroom when I saw two glowing pink eyes watching me. The white mouse was back.

"Squeakity," I told him, then in my haste, switched to human language. "I wish you'd help me with these cameras."

His eyes widened and nose twitched. "Which ones?" he asked.

I'm glad I was on solid footing because I sat back on my haunches like I'd been struck. "The…the ones in the bedrooms."

"I'll do the ones in the back," he told me, and dashed off.

Vibrating with adrenaline, I ran to the first bedroom, found the camera, and ripped it from its perch. Next, I ran to the second bedroom. The camera was hanging on its wires, having been removed from the duct tape. The white mouse was at the last camera, hovering next to the hole in the wall.

"Should we chew the wires now?" he asked.

I nodded. "How do you speak human?"

He ran his paw across his whiskers. "I was born and raised in a lab. They did a lot of…stuff…to me."

He sounded pitiful when he said that last bit,

which made me sad. "Well, why don't we chew up these wires, then we can get to know one another?"

Nodding, he picked up one of three lines and stuffed it in his mouth. It took exactly four bites before the camera hit bottom with a thud. I ran around to the bathroom wall and did my work. Chewing through the wires didn't take as long as running to each location. We met at Olivia's bedroom, all four cameras having been dispatched down the walls.

"Squeaks-squeaky?" I asked.

He shook his head. "I don't speak that language. I lost it all with the testing."

"I'm sorry. My name is Hazel. What's yours?"

"M Ten Ninety-Two."

"What kind of a name is that?"

"We all have names like that. F Nineteen Twelve was my mom. M Twenty Fifty-Three was the white in the next cage."

"The white mouse?"

"What's a mouse?" he asked.

"Umm, us." I pointed to him and me. "We are mice, mice being the plural of mouse."

"Is that so?" He closed his eyes. "I never knew."

"Olivia!" Brina called. "Your hair looks fine, let's go!"

I heard the jumble of voices and footsteps that

ended with a door slamming. The noise faded as the girls took the path away from the bungalow, supposedly toward the party. Glancing back at my new friend, I told him, "M Ten Ninety-Two is a big name. Can I just call you Em?"

He twitched his whiskers. "I guess…Hazel."

"Look, the girls have all left. Let's go exploring." I waved at him to follow me, then descended down the wall to the crack I had first entered, the crack where my family lived for so long. Creeping out, I sniffed the space, gazing around the room to make certain it was empty. Much like her bedroom at home, Olivia had semi-organized her space, hanging a couple of dresses in the closet and setting an open bag out for dirty clothes.

I was halfway across the bedroom floor when I glanced back to see if Em was following. He wasn't. Sighing, I turned to leave and jumped a mile straight up.

Em was before me, sitting on his haunches and cleaning his whiskers.

"Squeak!" I shouted, before remembering his disability. "I mean, catsnjammers, you startled me. Let's see what's in the kitchen."

I ran off, listening to his claws tapping the wood floor as he followed.

The rooms in this house were small compared to

my current home. At least Olivia's grandfather had done his best to reconfigure the common living areas by opening them into a single great room. I spent a few moments crossing the room toward the table. At the nearest leg, I stopped and listened for any sign of humans.

"Why are we stopping?" Em asked.

"Shh." I held my paw to his mouth. "Who knows if that Leo guy is still around?"

After a few moments of silence, we climbed the table leg to see what the girls had left. I knew for a fact that Olivia was not a fastidious housekeeper, and that the snacks on the porch earlier were probably now in the middle of the table—if they'd been moved at all.

FOUR

MY INSTINCTS WERE RIGHT, and I now surveyed the leftovers of the girls' afternoon snack-a-thon. Open bags of salty chips, boxes of crunchy crackers, slices of yellow cheese, creamy dips, all awaited me. And Em, I admitted. I dove into the cheese first, grabbing a slice and chewing on a morsel.

Em hopped onto the table and sat back, his front paws in the air and his head tilted back as if he questioned his own eyesight.

"What are you doing?"

"Eating." I held up a handful of hard, yellow deliciousness. "And when I'm full, I'm stuffing my face to take home snacks for later."

Em leaned forward to sniff. "What is it?"

"Are you kidding? Cheese. They say it's our favorite food, although I prefer Frosted Flakes."

"Cheese." His whiskers twitched. "Never heard of it."

"Where have you been?"

"In a dark place." His eyes drooped, losing their brightness. "We ate pellets. And this." He held up a cloth napkin and chewed a corner. "Mmm, Egyptian cotton."

"You ate napkins?"

"Is that what you call it?" He continued to nibble. "This is premium."

"Doesn't sound very tasty." I shoved a wedge of cheddar at him. "Try this."

He held it like it was a bomb, turning it over slowly and sniffing it several times before taking the smallest nibble. I watched his eyes open in surprise as he shoved the entire piece into his mouth.

"This tastes great!" he mumbled as he chewed.

I moved on to the crackers, then the chips, as Em followed, tasting each new treat before diving in and gorging himself. My stomach was feeling heavy, and I had just put a cracker in my cheek pouch, when I heard heavy boots and the garage door slamming.

"Come on, we gotta run." I scampered across the table and down the leg, stopping to look only when I was safe behind the refrigerator.

Em was not with me, and I hoped he had at least found shelter. Leo walked into the room, slightly swaying. I'd seen Olivia walk that way after coming in late from a party. Sometimes it was because her heels were too high, and sometimes it was because she drank too much. I checked Leo's shoes.

Drunk.

"Stupid witches." Leo grabbed the chips and dip, then staggered to the refrigerator and opened the door. "What they got to drink around here?" He pulled out a beer and slammed the fridge shut, leaning against it. "Stupid cameras, now I gotta dig through the walls and figure out what went wrong —hey!"

He was staring at the corner, and I knew what was there. Em. I looked to see my white mouse-friend cowering against the baseboard, his eyes looking frantically for escape. Leo stomped across the room.

"You chewed my camera wires!" Leo roared. "I'mma kick the crap outta you!"

There was no thinking to be done, no second guessing myself. I galloped to Em, putting myself between him and the caretaker.

"Raw-rrr!" I screamed. "Leave us alone!"

I've seen this reaction in humans when they hear me speak, but it never gets old. Leo stopped as if frozen, his left foot still behind him in mid-kick. His squinty eyes were stretched open, as was his thin-lipped mouth.

Grabbing my new friend, I scurried from the corner on three legs, dragging him along until he picked up the pace and ran with me.

"Do you think he noticed that you spoke to him?" Em asked.

I glanced over my shoulder to see the tall, thin man fall back into one of the kitchen chairs.

"Oh, yes," I said. "He noticed."

We reached Olivia's bedroom, ran through the crack, and I sighed in relief.

"Now what?" Em asked.

"What do you mean? What do you usually do?"

"Sit here in the dark, eat napkins, and feel lonely." He pulled a piece of fabric from the edge of the wall and held it out.

"Okay, not everything is called a 'napkin' but—never mind, come with me." I motioned for him to follow and wound my way to the outside wall, and the beach.

I trotted to the end of the porch and jumped into the sand. As I looked back, Em was standing at the edge of the porch, a look of alarm in his eyes.

"I can't," he said. "It's too big out here."

Fair enough, I thought, then I remembered what

my dad always told me. "It is a big world. But you only have to take small steps in it."

He stared at me for a few minutes, then spread his paws and leaped. I smiled and nodded, and we walked toward the sea together. The sun was well on its way to the water as I approached the shore, encouraging Em to join me. The tide was strong and high and foaming waves hurled themselves on the beach. I stuck my paws into the wet sand and let the water rush over them, feeling the grittiness disappear from underneath me.

Scampering away, I said, "Come on, Em, this is fun!"

He scanned the beach from his place further up the sand. "No, thank you, I'm fine here. This is fine. Just fine."

I was a little cross but tried to understand his discomfort. "I promise you'll be safe. Just come down here and touch the water."

Em twitched his whiskers and took a step toward the shore, stopped, twitched, and stepped again, stopped again, and continued toward me. It took my entire breath and body to not yell for him to hurry up. After what seemed like a week, he was by my side.

"Okay, now plant your paws," I told him. "And

let the water surround them and move the sand. Then jump away."

"If you say so," he said, looking unsure.

We stood together, toes buried, as the waves curled around us.

"Jump!" I yelled and gave him a tug backward. Our feet hit the firm ground as the water left the shore. We repeated this several times, each time eliciting a bigger, more relaxed smile from Em.

"This is fun," he said and hopped back to the wet sand to await the next wave.

"That's a little far." I could see that he'd ventured beyond the last waterline, and I could also see that the tide was coming in, so I ran down to pull him to safer ground just as the water returned.

This wave came in a little stronger than the last and rose to our bellies, lifting us out of the sand and pulling us both out to sea.

"Oh, no, help!" shrieked Em.

"Turn around," I said, pushing him toward the shore, "and paddle hard."

We both turned and swept our legs against the water that kept sucking us toward the open ocean. I tilted my head toward the sky to keep breathing, and I could see Em's nose bobbing in and out of the water, sputtering with each dunking. We were barely holding our positions against the tidal pull when I saw the water whip Em around to face the ocean. I grabbed his tail and kept swimming with three legs.

At the point I thought my body might collapse, the new wave arrived, cutting under the retreating one and sending us sailing to the beach. Em managed to turn around in time to slide in, head-first, his nose digging a trough as he went. One last surge of water lifted me and slammed me on top of him.

I was exhausted but knew another wave was coming, so I grabbed Em's ear. "We gotta get out of the surf."

We crawled together until we hit dry sand and flopped onto our bellies. It was quiet, except for the roar of the next wave. Thankfully, we were out of its reach.

"Hazel." Em's voice was quiet and as tired as his body. "Was that fun?"

I would have laughed if I had the energy. "No, that was not fun. I'm sorry. The water does creep up on you."

A loud voice interrupted our recovery. "Get your hands off me, you perv!"

FIVE

I LOOKED up in time to see heavy boots stomping toward me and Em. Scurrying away, I had just enough time to reach out for Em's tail and pull him back to the wet sand.

"But I do not want to have fun with the water again!" he wailed.

I shushed him. "Did you want to get stepped on?"

We both looked up at the boot that just missed us, and the person it was attached to. Leo was chasing after Olivia, who was stumbling back toward the beach house. I wasn't certain if she was drunk or just having a hard time walking in the sand with her wedge sandals. She was scowling and glancing over her shoulder.

"I thought I was clear that you are to leave my

friends and me alone," she spat.

Leo kept up his pursuit. "And I thought I was clear. Your daddy owes me. Call him and ask what you have to do to keep me from telling certain people certain things."

"I don't care." She stopped and faced him. "My dad's not going to pimp me out, no matter what you have over him."

The handyman took a step toward her, and she brought her knee up hard in between his legs. He doubled forward with a groan, as if all the air had been pushed from him.

"Don't mess with me, old man." Her voice was so flat it frightened me. "I'm young and rich, and I can make you disappear. Daddy wouldn't have to worry about who you tell what."

She turned and went to the beach house as I sat on my haunches, trying to process what just happened. Leo left at some point, but I was so busy staring at the door she'd disappeared into, I didn't notice where he went.

"Hazel…Hazel." Em's voice finally permeated my ears. "What are you looking at?

I shook my head and pointed. "That girl lives in my bedroom at home. I've seen her act like a princess before and a mean girl plenty of times, but I've never seen her threaten anyone with murder."

Em looked unimpressed. "So?"

"It's a big thing when a human threatens to kill another human. And I've never even heard her say the words, not even when she's been madder than the cat when he can't catch me."

"Oh. The humans at the lab said it a lot." He sat back and looked at the sky. "James kept taking Bill's beakers, so Bill would yell, 'do it again and I'll kill you.' Then Bill would use up all the swabs and not get more, so James would yell, 'I'm not your maid service, restock the bloody swabs or I'll poison your tea.'"

"Wow, they don't sound very nice."

Em lowered his eyes, and I could see the pain in his drooped whiskers. "They weren't."

"Well, let's get you to a better life in a better place," I told him. "I'm hungry again, how about you?"

We had ventured far from the house, so the sun had well set by the time we reached the porch. I was scampering up the bleached wood when the door flung wide, and Olivia raced out into the night. She was breathing heavily—I could hear her panting. I let her pass before proceeding to the house. There was no need to scare her at the moment.

At a small hole to squeeze through, I turned to Em, who had stayed behind me the entire trip. "I think that's what Olivia calls having a bug up her butt."

"That doesn't sound pleasant for the bug."

"No, it's not literally a—never mind." I entered the house and proceeded along the baseboard, on my way to the kitchen again. I stopped at the door with my usual caution. The food was still there, as I could smell, but maybe a human was there, too.

"Why are we waiting?" Em asked. "There are no lights on. When the humans leave, it becomes dark."

"True, but…" I whispered, with a feeling that something wasn't right. "Just because the lights are out, it doesn't mean that no one's home."

A heavy thud got our attention, along with a low, moaning protest. The noise was coming from Olivia's room. I turned toward the sound and crept forward.

"Where are you going?" Em pulled on my tail.

"Aren't you curious?"

"No, that wasn't part of my training."

Shaking his paw from me, I trotted to the edge of the bedroom and slipped under the door. Two figures wrestled in the darkness, humans. Leo was fighting with someone—or were they?

He was leaning into the other person, wrapping his arms around them and moving his hands up and down while they pushed against him and protested.

"Nooo, get off me." It was a woman, but there

was so little light and so much grappling, I couldn't tell who it was. Nothing about their voice sounded unique from the others.

"You know you've wanted this, ever since I seen you today," Leo growled.

As they moved toward the window, where I could get a better view, I heard Leo make a funny grunt, gasp, and gurgle. The woman stepped back, and Leo fell to the floor.

I ran to the corner and turned to look again, just in time to see the door open and the woman's shadow vanish from the room. At the entrance, a faint white shape with two red eyes peered inside.

My immediate thought was to run over to Em to protect him from Leo again, but as I ran past, Leo did not look up from his place on the ground. I stopped and turned to regard the man.

"What are you doing?" Em whispered. "You're too close to him."

"Shhh." I tiptoed up to Leo's outstretched hand and sniffed at him.

Mice have a good sense of smell, and among mice, I have an exceptional nose. What I smelled of the Leo on the floor did not smell quite like the Leo that chased me and Em. I recognized his new smell—he was dead.

SIX

"HE WON'T CAPTURE US," I told Em. "I think that woman killed him."

"Squee!" Em squeaked and put his paws over his mouth.

"Sounds like you're learning to speak mouse," I said. "But come look at what he has in his hand."

The stiffness of death had not entered his body yet, but his outstretched hand contained a scrap of something. Em, in his usual caution, took forever and a year to crawl over to me before stretching his neck out and sniffing the scrap.

"It's a napkin."

"No, not all fabric—" I began and checked myself. This was not the time for an English lesson. "Do you recognize it?"

"Sure," he said with an exaggerated twitch. "One

hundred percent rayon. I can smell it, but I can't taste it. Gives me seizures."

"Ray-yawn," I repeated. "Do all clothes have that?"

"What are clothes?"

I frowned and thought. "Let's go to the kitchen. I'd like to know more about what you did in the lab, and we'll need food for that."

By the time our stomachs were bulging, and our cheek pouches stuffed, I had taught Em about the different types of "napkins," and he had told me about the kind of work they made him do.

"I guess it wasn't as bad as being a tester mouse, where they poked you all day with needles to give you cancer, or a rabbit—they get stuff rubbed into their eyes. I only got poked sometimes. But I can tell the different make up of any nap—*fabric* they fed me or poked into my skin. Rayon's the only thing that made me sick."

"Doesn't that mean the humans stop making things out of rayon?"

He shook his head. "No, they just added other stuff to it until I stopped having seizures." He nodded toward the bedroom. "That must be from something old."

A light popped on in the doorway and laughter

entered the room, along with generally loud body movements.

"Ohmygod I'm still kinda hungry." Olivia's words slurred together. "I'm goin' ta kitchen."

I grabbed Em and dashed down the table leg and into the corner. The kitchen light blazed to life as we huddled together.

"Why aren't we going back to our den?" he asked.

"In Olivia's room?" I stared at him. "With Leo's body?"

"Oh. Yeah."

We stood very still, hoping that four drunk girls wouldn't see us. Olivia reached into the bag and extracted a large, crinkled chip, which she scraped through the hummus.

"I'm get inna my PJs," she mumbled as she munched and staggered to her room.

Em nudged me, his eyes wide with anticipation. I felt much the same.

"OH MY GOD aren't they cute?" Ashley's voice was loud and high. I looked up to see her bending down, looking at me and Em. "One of them is albino. Do you think he's somebody's pet?"

She reached her hand out to Em but froze when we all heard the scream. Ashley jumped up as Olivia ran to the kitchen doorway.

"He's dead he's dead ohmygod he's dead." Olivia was nearly chanting. She didn't seem as drunk anymore.

A cacophony of questions from the other girls filled the air, so loud that I put my paws over my ears. I felt a nudge on my shoulder. Em nodded at the fridge, and I agreed. We both ran behind the large humming box, into a slit in the drywall. I scrambled up the nearest wooden beam.

"Where are you going?" Em stood at the bottom but did not follow.

"Olivia's room. I want to see what happens now."

There weren't any cracks or holes in the ceiling, but an overhead light hung down on a chain. There was no bulb in the socket, so no worries about being lit. I settled into the translucent bowl and peered over the edge.

Ashley stood over Leo's body, looking at him from all angles. Olivia was near the dresser, her head buried in Brina's shoulder while Claire stood in the doorway, her skin pale and her hair moist around her temples.

"What should we do?" Ashley asked, reaching for the dead man.

"First of all, we don't touch anything, including him," Brina ordered. "Then we call the police."

"The police?" Olivia looked at her, eyes wide with

panic. "There's a dead body in my room and we should call the police?"

Brina stroked Olivia's shoulder. "Livvy, it's for the best. We can't exactly hide this."

"Why can't we?" Claire remained by the door, as if she might bolt at any second.

"Because a man is dead and his killer needs to be caught," Brina told her.

"They're going to look at him in this room, and finger one of us," Claire said. "Much easier than looking for the actual killer."

Ashley stood up. "Well…if we were going to hide this, how would we do it?"

"Ashley!" Olivia surprised me with her scold. "He was murdered. Even a perv deserves justice."

Claire shook her head. "But does he really?"

A knock at the door startled everyone, including me. The girls looked at each other, each voice talking over three others.

"Who can it be?" "Someone go answer." "No, maybe they'll leave." "What do we do?"

At the second, louder rapping, Olivia pushed away from Brina and straightened her shoulders. "I'll go."

I dashed up the light fixture and over the ceiling to the front door, shimmying down the beam to poke myself out of a sliver of cracked drywall. Olivia opened the door to two men in uniforms. I couldn't help but wonder if someone had already called the police—their timing was impeccable.

"Good morning, I'm Officer Alvarez," the tall, broad man said. "And this is my partner, Officer Boyd. Just wanted to introduce ourselves around the neighborhood. With summer starting, there are a lot of new folks around here and we want you to know this area is safe."

Olivia stood silent. I expected her to send them away and call Daddy. Some story would be concocted, and she would eventually walk away unbothered by this. And Leo would never be spoken of again.

I couldn't let her get away with it. In my most entitled young girl voice, I yelled, "Officer, in the bedroom, please help us!"

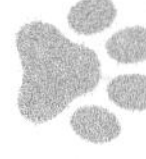

SEVEN

OLIVIA WHIPPED around to see which one of her gal pals had called out, while the young policeman moved through the doorway, putting his arm out to block anything Olivia might do to stop him. His partner followed, talking into a small box on his shoulder as he walked.

Scurrying across the beams, I reached the bedroom as Officer Alvarez herded the young women out.

"We need to clear the room, Ladies," he told them. "We don't want to disturb the scene."

I followed them, crossing the roof beams to a step-down that opened to the living area.

Olivia and Ashley sat on separate ends of the sofa, letting the overstuffed leather cradle them.

Brina slipped into a tulip chair, her half-lidded eyes revealing her boredom, and Claire propped herself on a stool at the kitchen bar. She chewed her lip and crossed her legs, wiggling her right foot.

"All right," Alvarez said, flipping a page in his notebook. "While we wait for the detectives and the CSU, why don't I get your names? I'll need to see your IDs."

"Olivia Bent, and this house belongs to my family." She rose casually and strolled to the kitchen counter to retrieve her purse.

The other three dug their licenses from their bags and handed them, one by one, to the officer, who wrote the information in his book.

"Do any of you know the deceased?" he asked.

The girls all looked at each other, shrugging.

"Yes," Claire finally admitted. "He's the caretaker, Leo."

"Leo what?" Officer Alvarez asked.

Three girls turned and looked at Olivia.

"How should I know?" she said before turning to the policemen with a sigh. "Leo's just the caretaker." She glanced toward the end of the hall. "I mean, he *was* the caretaker."

"Leo Carter," Officer Boyd held up a wallet as he entered the room. "Forty-nine, lives off of Main and Adams. Expired driver's license."

Officer Alvarez nodded. "Did any of you see what happened?"

I could hear an army of footsteps outside, getting closer. None of the humans looked toward the door until it squeaked open. Alvarez jerked his head up and smiled in recognition.

"Detective Rogers," he greeted the woman. "I was just getting some preliminary information."

"Thanks, Tom." A tall, dark-haired woman entered the room. "What've we got?"

"This way." Alvarez moved to the hall. "Boyd, can you watch the witnesses?"

Officer Boyd was a short, square young man with extraordinary blond hair and blue eyes. "Is he an albino like you?" I asked.

Em shrugged. "Maybe, but I doubt it. His eyes aren't red."

"Stay here and watch them," I told Em. "I'm going to see what the police are saying about Leo."

"Why?"

"Because—" An answer eluded me. "Because I'm curious."

"You know curiosity killed the cat."

"And I'm not a cat." I shivered. "Ew."

I left him to run back to the bedroom. Why did I want to hear the police? Why did I care that Leo died, or how he died, or who killed him? My only answer was that not knowing made my skin itch.

As I scampered, I could hear the rush of female voices busily denying seeing anything, hearing anything, or even being near the house.

In the bedroom, two women in neat dark trousers and light blouses stood over poor Leo. There was a young man in the corner, riffling through a large kit and pulling out gloves. He handed some to the women.

The tallest one, Detective Rogers, reached down to pull Leo's shirt collar back with her gloved fingers, moving on to turn over his hands, and roll Leo over enough to see the dark stain on his chest.

"I'd say it wasn't premeditated," she said.

"Possible self-defense?" The other woman was shorter, darker skinned, and muscular.

Rogers nodded. "Boyd says his name's Leo Carter, forty-nine."

"Carter?" Her partner asked. "Aren't the guys in Narcotics following this guy?"

"They were. Could never find anything on him so they cut him loose." Rogers studied the room. "Doesn't look like much of a struggle, nothing toppled. Jerry, go ahead and dust the furniture for prints, but concentrate on the body and everything immediately surrounding it."

"Sure thing," the CSU officer said.

The detective nudged her partner. "Well, Neva, let's go see if one of these girls had an accidental tussle with Mr. Carter."

EIGHT

I WATCHED Jerry take out his camera and take many photos, so many photos, from every angle possible. He moved around the room, bending to pick up pieces of this and that, placing them in baggies and writing numbers on everything.

Curiosity overwhelmed me and I scampered to the corner where I could ease down the wall and emerge unobserved. I grabbed the wood framing with my claws and crawled to the floor. A small hole in the baseboard allowed me to pop out into the dark closet.

I immediately fell into a mound of fabric. The cloth swallowed me and I clamored my way out of all the folds. Apparently, the material's rustling caught Jerry's attention—the next thing I knew, a flashlight was blinding me.

"Hello, Buddy," Jerry said.

He seemed so friendly I almost answered him. But I knew it would be too awkward, so I ran to a far corner and hid under the bed.

His light lingered on the fabric, and I watched him pull the rumpled clothing from the floor. It was a red shirt and looked suspiciously like the scrap of material Leo clutched. Something about it bothered me. I watched Jerry take more photos before getting out another bag and scribbling on it.

What had begun as an interesting activity to observe was quickly boring, so I ran back to the closet and up to the rafters, where I could access the living room. I wanted to see what the girls were telling the detectives. I found Em on one of the beams, looking down through the overhead light fixture.

Sidling up to him, I whispered, "What's going on so far?"

He jumped sideways and looked at me. "Don't scare me like that."

"Sorry." I twitched my whiskers. "Did you see who stabbed Leo? It was so dark in the room, I'm pretty sure it was one of these girls, but which one?"

Em shook his head. "I didn't see, either."

I sat back. "I don't know why I'm so curious

about this. One more dead human is one less problem for me."

"What are you going to do now?" Em asked. He was chewing on something.

"Enjoy my vacation, I guess—what are you eating?"

"Napkins—I mean, fabric, right?" He held up a familiar-looking piece of material.

"Is that from Leo's hand?"

"No, I told you that fabric gives me seizures. I found this in one of the closets." He closed his eyes as he nibbled. "There's about forty percent cotton and a splash of spandex in this."

I sighed. "Wouldn't you rather eat cheese?"

"Probably." He shrugged. "Cheese tastes better but this tastes familiar."

I told him about Jerry's find in the closet. "I'm betting that shirt has a hole that matches the scrap in Leo's hand." I rocked back on my haunches to think. "You know, it's funny. Olivia's clothes are all stored away, and she's got a bag set up as a hamper. Why'd she toss her shirt in the corner? I don't even remember seeing a red shirt in her luggage."

"Why do you care about that? They're just humans."

I gazed down at the detectives, who were now

standing in the living area. The taller one, Rogers, flipped through Officer Alvarez' notes, then passed them to Detective Neva. "Because the longer the police are here trying to solve the crime, the busier this place will be and the less relaxing. I'm trying to take a vacation!"

"I don't know what a vacation is, but why don't you wait for everyone to go to bed, then take one from the pantry?"

I put both paws over my mouth to keep from laughing out loud. "No, a vacation is when you go somewhere to enjoy yourself."

"I don't know what *enjoy* is, either." He wiped his whiskers.

"Sorry." I didn't know what else to say. I could hear Jerry in the bedroom, still clomping about. "We won't be able to get to our home in the wall for a while. Why don't we find a space behind the cabinets in the kitchen to take a nap? At least we'll be close to the food."

Em nodded and turned. We crawled along the beams to the kitchen area, shimmied down the wood and emerged from the wall into the back of the cabinet under the sink. There was no door to this storage, just a small curtain, yellow with pops of daisies. Light filtered through the fabric, making a hazy landscape of bottles, cans, and sponges.

"Napkins!" Em ran for the curtain, but I stopped him.

"No napkin eating here," I said. "These curtains have to hide us, at least for a bit."

I hadn't noticed the chaotic level of human conversation until Detective Rogers' voice cut through them. My curiosity overruled my good sense and I peeked out of the curtain to watch.

"Ladies, let's get back on track. Ashley, you were saying there was animosity between Miss Bent and Mr. Carter?"

"Oh, no, Detective." Ashley stood up, waving her hands. "That's not what we meant at all."

"Yes, it is," Brina told him, then turned to her friends. "Withholding information will go badly. My dad's a criminal defense lawyer, trust me on this."

"Miss Bent?" Rogers said. "Have anything to say?"

From my vantage point, I saw Olivia's face turn tomato-red and she shook her head slowly.

The detective sighed and nodded at her partner. "Detective Smythe is going to escort you to the patio now. I will call you in one at a time for more questioning."

Brina nodded and smiled knowingly at the others. "We're not supposed to be coordinating our stories."

"As a matter of fact, miss, we can begin with you." Smythe gestured toward the table. "Have a seat, please."

The other girls shuffled out of the kitchen, so I closed the curtain and returned to the back corner. "This is bad," I told Em.

"I don't understand."

"Olivia will be their suspect."

"So?"

"So if she isn't allowed to leave, I don't have a ride home." I sat back. "I mean, other than that, I don't care, except she didn't do it. We saw her leave."

"But who would we tell?" he asked.

I passed my paw over my right ear. "The police, of course."

Em stared at me, silent.

"Look, I am aware we're mice. I don't even talk to humans, and I've never been tempted to do anything nice for Olivia—she's a spoiled brat. But right is right, and there's got to be a way to tell the police what we saw, without having them freak out."

"Or squish us."

"Or squish us—us?" Now it was my turn to stare. "When did I ask you to help me?"

"You didn't. But what else am I going to do, if I'm not in a cage being fed pellets and napkins?"

"Okay. Let's find a way back into the wall. I've got one idea for getting the detectives' attention."

Feeling along the baseboards, I found a place we could squeeze through and soon we were traveling along the beams. I could hear Jerry in Brina's room, so I headed there. On my way, I heard Olivia's voice from the patio. I paused to listen.

"I don't care if he's in conference, tell Daddy it's an extreme emergency."

A woman's voice replied from the speaker. "Yes, Miss Bent, but he will not be pleased."

Music played from her phone, but I could still hear her impatient nails clicking against the exterior stucco. "Come on, Daddy. I need you," she whispered. I had never heard her sound so plaintive, like a child needing comfort.

"This had better be important," a deep male voice boomed.

The child who needed her Daddy disappeared, replaced by cold-blooded sarcasm. "You tell me. Leo's been murdered."

There was no response, so she continued. "Did you hear me, Daddy? Leo was stabbed to death, in the beach house, in my room. I may be the number one suspect. Is that important enough?"

"Leo Carter is dead?" Her father had found his

voice. "Are you certain? Never mind, of course you're certain. So...Leo is dead...stabbed...police are there...why do they think you might have done it?"

"Because he was stabbed in my room—were you listening? And after the blowup I had with him, well, correction—blowups, plural, the police know he wasn't my favorite person. Why didn't you fire him when I told you to?"

"It's complicated, Sweetheart. How did the police know about your fights with him?"

Olivia sighed. "Brina. Lawyer's daughter, blah, blah, don't hide the truth. She ratted me out."

"Brina. That makes sense."

The way he said it made me curious. "I mean, I guess it makes sense," I mused, "about her having a lawyer for a dad, but he said it like it means more."

"What are you blabbering about?" Em had snuck up next to me again.

"Sorry, did I say it out loud? I was talking to myself, I guess."

"Daddy." Olivia the child was back. "What do I do?"

"Let me call our attorney," Daddy told her, his voice calm and reassuring. "In the meantime, do not speak with the police. This is all going to be okay, you'll see. Even better than okay. This is going to be the best thing that ever happened to this family."

I sat, rubbing my whiskers. The best thing that ever happened? I remembered Claire's musing. Did Leo have something on dear old Dad? I turned to Em. "We may have two mysteries to solve."

NINE

"I STILL DO NOT SEE why we have to solve anything."

"Look, you're the one who doesn't have anything better to do, besides eat fabric and mope. The more we help the police, the faster they solve the crime and the sooner they leave. It's a win-win."

"What do we win?"

"Peace," I said, "and a ride home." I motioned for him to follow. "Let's go to Brina's room. I need to get Jerry's attention."

Jerry was still in the room, poking about with gloved hands. He was at the dresser, moving things around and opening drawers.

I looked down the drywall, where Leo's camera had fallen. It was still there, wedged against the bottom, and I wished we had only chewed the wires, leaving the cameras for the detectives to find.

Figuring to give Jerry what I could, I ran down the stud to the wires and pulled until I had enough of the chewed ends to shove through the hole.

"What are you doing?" Em stood above me on the ceiling beam.

"Giving them something to investigate." I looked down at Jerry, who was still bagging things and writing.

His back was to me, so I first tried scratching at the wall with my nails. He didn't even look up. Next was squeaking. I burst out my loudest, most staccato stream of noise but he did not move, and I began to wonder if he wore ear buds.

There was nothing left to do if I wanted him to see these wires. I cleared my throat and took a deep breath before putting my face up to the hole.

"OH MY GAWD!" I yelled.

That got his attention. The CSU officer jumped, looking around for the source of the noise. Detective Rogers ran into the room.

"What was that?"

"I don't know," Jerry said. "But look." He tugged on the wires, and I slunk out of his way.

"Could be a lighting fixture," Rogers said. "But that hole is in such an odd place, I'm betting we've had unwanted surveillance in this room. Maybe all these rooms. See if you can find what these wires were attached to. Find out from Miss Bent if there is a surveillance system."

Em smiled at me. "Good idea."

We climbed back up to the roof beam. "I'm getting hungry again. Let's go back to the pantry."

Following the attic's network of planks, we found the kitchen and scurried down to where the food was stored. I introduced Em to peanuts and chocolate donuts, and we proceeded to gorge ourselves.

"I bed dinkin," Em said through his mouthful of yeasty dough. "Bout dat rayon shirt in Olivia's room."

"Yes." I nodded, swallowing. "Something bothers me about it."

"It's so old, much older than her other clothes."

"So?"

Em shook his head. "Humans wear similar napkins—er, fabric. I learned that listening to the humans in the lab. Humans are naked and the feel of clothes is very important to them. If a human wears cotton it's because they prefer the feel of cotton."

His words began to make sense in my brain. "So what you're saying is—"

"That's not Olivia's shirt."

"Not only that," I said. "It was tossed in her

closet. Why would she toss it in her closet when she had a bag to use for her dirty clothes."

I turned to him as we both said, "Someone else put it there."

"But who?" he asked.

"I don't know…" I chewed on another nut. "If humans like to wear the same kind of fabric, maybe we see which girl has more of this—ray yawn—in her suitcase?"

"Okay." He closed his eyes as he chewed. "After one more bite of donut."

We followed the beams back to Brina's room and scrambled down. There was no sound, so I peeked out of a crack in the baseboard. The room was small but tastefully decorated to look as large as possible with pale walls and blonde furniture, and storage cubicles to keep it all tidied.

Brina's suitcase had exploded all over the space. There wasn't a patch of bed or floor to be seen under the outfits.

"No one's here." I sighed at the amount of work. "Looks like she brought her entire wardrobe. Let's see how much we can get through."

We crawled down to the sea of fabric, and I followed Em around the mess. "Whew! I may not be able to taste ray-yawn, but her perfume is very strong."

"Is that the smell?" Em asked. "Purr Foom? I thought she just smelled funny for a human."

I chuckled. "You have a lot to learn about the world."

After climbing through blouses and skirts, we sat in the corner and surveyed the landscape.

"There is nothing even partially rayon here," Em said. "This is all luxury fabric, and new. Even the silks have state-of-the-art processing."

"So Brina was not the one. Next room, next girl." I stopped. "Claire and Ashley are sharing the room. I'll see where Jerry is."

I checked the living area. Brina had been brought to the living room, where she sat with Detective Rogers. She had draped her small frame gracefully in the tulip chair, ankles crossed as she slowly arched and straightened both feet. I suppose it could be a sign of a casual stretch, but her tightened facial muscles read nervous energy to me.

"He wasn't the nicest man to any of us," She was telling the detective. "Yes, Olivia called her dad and wanted him fired—I mean, he threw our suitcases in our rooms and broke several things. But none of us ever wished him dead—at least not out loud to the others."

"Why don't you walk me through your day?"

Rogers said. There water bottles on the table between them and she was scribbling on a notepad.

"I'm assuming you mean after we arrived here. Otherwise, I spent my morning throwing things in a bag and driving to Olivia's."

Rogers smiled. "So you threw things in a bag but you were mad that Leo threw your bags in your room?"

"Figure of speech, Detective." Brina scowled. "He broke my bottle of eye cream , and I had to wash all of my other toiletries, plus the inside of my bag. It was extremely messy and expensive."

Moving on, I found the three other girls with Detective Smythe on the patio. Four cell phones were piled atop each other on the table. The girls sat silently, staring at one another.

"C'mon." I grabbed Em by the ear and motioned for him to follow. "We have a quick chance to look through their bedroom before Jerry comes in."

Claire was much more organized than Brina. Clothes were hung in the closet and put into the various wicker baskets on the dresser. I immediately crawled up to the baskets. As much as I love cheese, wicker has always appealed to me, in both its flavor and its crunch. I couldn't resist a nibble.

Ashley's side of the room was the neatest of the girls. One small suitcase sat in the corner, opened to reveal shelves of carefully folded clothes. The dresser contained two caddies, one with shampoo and soap, and another with makeup and perfume.

I made a quick scamper through the closet, drawers and twin bed, but found nothing.

Em stood at the end of Claire's bed, his nose twitching sideways, pointing. "I think we found the rayon wearer."

Then he fell over.

Rushing to his side, I grabbed his tail and dragged him to the middle of the room, a feat I accomplished on sheer adrenaline. He was stiff and silent for several minutes and I feared I would have to leave him here. We mice do not have much in the way of funerals or honoring the dead.

I tapped on his face to see if I could wake him.

"Get up, Em," I pleaded. "I can't drag you any farther."

His eyes fluttered open, and he stared at me, his body still motionless.

"What the hell?" I asked.

"Sorry," he whispered. "Seizure."

"I thought you only had those when you tasted the fabric."

"I wanted to make certain."

"Well don't do it again. That was supremely scary." I looked at the clothing he'd pointed to. It was a pair of red shorts, the same red as the shirt, draped across the foot of Claire's bed. "These may be part of a set. We need to get the police in here."

A squeal filled the hallway, and I looked up to see Ashley staring at us in horror. I ran a few steps from Em, felt badly about leaving him so vulnerable, and turned back to defend him. If I couldn't scare the girl from us, I could always threaten to run up her leg.

"OhMyGawd did you talk?" she asked, her mouth open in awe.

I stood in front of Em, considering my response. I had vowed never to speak to humans, but—

"Maybe," I told her.

She sat down on the area rug, her legs crossed. "How is this possible?"

I shrugged. "It's complicated."

"I'm sorry about your little friend." She gestured to Em. "Did he die of fright?"

"He's not dead. He calls it a 'see-shure.'"

"Oh, a seizure. My sister has those. Mild epilepsy."

I had no idea what that word meant, so I changed the subject. "If you'll pardon me, I thought you were afraid of mice."

"I am—or at least I was. When you spoke, though…that was nuts."

"Yeah. Nuts." I heard Em behind me, stirring.

"Well, if you'll excuse me, my friend is waking up. We need to be disappearing into the wall."

I grabbed Em by the whiskers and pulled him toward the wall, to find a crack to squeeze into. Em was conscious but groggy and came along willingly.

"Oh, don't go," Ashley said. "Stay and talk to me."

I didn't answer but waved a paw and continued to steer Em. I flattened myself to scoot under. Em had fully awakened, looked up at the girl, and bolted, leaving me there to stare at my new friend.

"Thanks," I said and ran after Em.

TEN

I CAUGHT up with him in the ceiling above the kitchen.

"What was that?" he asked. "First you tell me not to trust humans, then you talk to them?"

"I know, I can't explain." I searched for something reasonable to tell him, but I didn't understand it either. "Apparently, she likes me when I speak like her. Maybe she's not like the others."

"Then tell her what you know and let's leave. Go to another house."

"Another house?" I was astounded at the idea. Yes, I wanted to be near the ocean, but I always thought that meant living in the beach house I knew, the house my family knew. Where else was there to go?

"I been thinking," Em said. "When I first got here,

I was so scared. I stayed in the house, mostly in that room. Now that I've been to the porch and the ocean, and eaten cheese, I feel like I want to see more."

"Then go." I gestured toward the outside. "See more."

"But I can't go without you, Hazel. You're the only mouse I know who speaks my language."

He was right. But did I want to see more?

"Ashley may want to talk to us, but I don't think she's the person to tell about Claire's shorts," I said. "We need to make the police aware." He shot me a cross look. "Okay, I need to make the police aware."

"How do you propose we do that?"

"I don't know." I stroked my whiskers and smoothed my fur. "Stay here. If you could find a way to point out the red shorts, do it!" I ran over the beams to the living area, where I found a pinpoint of light in between the ceiling and an overhead fixture.

Brina and Rogers had not changed positions. The young woman was telling the detective she didn't know anything or see anything or especially not hear anything.

"I'm not certain why I'm even talking to you," she said. "My father is a lawyer in L.A. you know."

"You are correct," Rogers told her. "Our conversation is strictly voluntary, although I would think you'd want to answer routine questions to help find who did this. But if you feel more secure under your dad's protection, feel free to call him."

I could hear the anxiety-riddled bravado in Brina's voice as she said, "I have a call in to his office. I'm sure he'll be calling soon."

Jerry burst into the room, his arms full. "I got cameras, Detective."

"Where were they?" Rogers asked.

"All the bedrooms plus the bathroom."

"What?!" Brina stood, her face flushed. "Of all the —whoever murdered him deserves a medal!"

"Now, Ms. Templeton," the detective warned and turned to Jerry. "Let's try to find what those cameras were hooked to."

"Detective?" Olivia was standing at the kitchen door. "Excuse me—I've been in these clothes since last night." She pointed down to her dress, a short white bit of material wrapped tightly around her.

"Spandex by the smell of it," Em said.

"Maybe I could get a change of clothes out of my room?" she continued.

The officer frowned. "Boyd!" he shouted. "Miss Bent is coming in to get a change of clothes." He nodded to Olivia. "Officer Boyd will *chaperone* you."

I ran to Olivia's room and slipped into the small closet. Her clothes were all neatly hung, organized by garment type and color. It was different from her closet at home, where clothes were barely hung at all. The closet door in this old house never closed all the way so I could see through the crack easily.

Leo's body had been removed, no doubt by one of the several people in uniform who had been traipsing in and out. I balanced on the rod that held the hangers.

Officer Boyd stepped away from the door to obscure my view just as Olivia opened the closet and reached in for a blue pinstriped romper that was on the hanger I was straddling. In my attempt to scatter away from her hand, I lost my balance and fell into the romper. Before I knew it, I was clinging to the inside of the back collar as she swung the hanger on her way to the bathroom to change.

Once in the bathroom, I tried to extricate myself from the fabric as she slipped her legs into the outfit, then her arms, and began to button the front. By now, I had fallen to the elastic waist and was trying to find a way out. I looked up to see a gap between the armhole and her shoulder and took my chance.

"Eeeaahhoooaaa!"

I'm not certain if Olivia was screaming or yodeling, but by the way she was gyrating, I guessed that she wasn't happy. She opened her top enough for me to escape, but there was no place to leap to, so I had to run down the outside of her clothes, slide down her calf and run to the bathroom cabinet.

"Sorry! Sorry! Sorry!" I yelped as I ran, and she continued to scream.

"Wait—" She half-screamed before composing herself. "Wait. Little mouse, is that you?"

I shoved myself into the corner, panting and looking for a hole to disappear into.

Olivia looked at her reflection. "Am I losing it like my Aunt Ginny?"

Let her wonder if she was crazy. There was no reason for me to answer. She was spoilt, entitled, and wanted me dead. I sat quietly out of sight, watching her examine her face.

"I know I heard someone say, 'Sorry.'" She continued to turn this way and that, examining herself. "But I do look like Auntie, and I'm about the same age as when she started hearing voices." She backed away from the mirror, looking at the floor. "Maybe I did kill Leo and I just don't remember."

It was one thing to let her think she was crazy. It was quite another to let her take the rap for Leo's murder.

"I said it." My high voice echoed through the small room. "And no, you didn't kill Leo."

"Where are you?" Olivia looked around. "And who are you?"

"Down here." I stepped from the corner. "Don't freak out."

She was silent for such a long moment, I thought she'd been struck mute. At last, she pointed and whispered, "You're the mouse from my room."

"Yes."

Her finger kept pointing, although it shook viciously. "How-how-how…?"

I decided to be helpful. "How do I speak English?" I asked with a bit of a smile. "It is a long story about a lightning strike, but I've been able to understand and speak human tongue since my birth."

She sat down on the gray tile floor—at least, I think she sat. It's possible she just collapsed. I stood far enough away to keep her from squishing me.

"Why are you talking to me now?" She frowned. "I mean, after all this time."

"Because I know you didn't kill Leo. I saw you leave." I told her everything I'd seen and heard up to that point, even about Leo's hidden cameras.

"Gross!" was her only comment.

We were interrupted by the sound of Officer Boyd's voice in the hallway.

"Sargeant Alvarez, I found something."

ELEVEN

I SAT UP, my ears perked for listening.

"Let's see," Alvarez said.

"Stay here," I told Olivia, and shimmied through a small crack in the cabinet, found a hole, and hurried up the wood frame to the ceiling, where Em waited.

"These were under the mattress." The officer held up something shiny. "The tip caught my eye when Ms. Bent turned the light on."

It was a pair of scissors, striped with blood.

"Take them to Detective Rogers. She'll want to take the Bent woman in for more questioning," Alvarez told him.

"No!" I shouted before Em could clamp his paws across my mouth.

The humans below us stopped talking. I could see

Alvarez holding his hand up as if to encourage Boyd's silence. They both scanned the room. For the first time in my life, I wanted to run from the ceiling, leap to the dresser and tell them what I knew.

Em stopped me. "Why would they listen to a mouse?"

"You are correct," I whispered. "But we need to do something."

"I believe we can help most by pointing the police in the right direction here."

I nodded. "Hopefully. I'll be right back."

"Where are you going?"

"To tell Olivia not to worry." I dashed toward the kitchen. "We're on the case."

It was a new adventure, this talking to humans.

I found her sitting on the edge of the tub, wiggling her foot and checking her phone.

"Come on, Daddy," she told it, "pick up."

Creeping to the center of the room, I stopped and sat up. "Um…Olivia?"

"I don't understand." She fiddled with her phone. "Daddy's not answering."

Just when I felt badly, she made me remember why I didn't like her. She had raised self-absorption into an art form. "Olivia, I need you to know the police just found a pair of bloody scissors under your mattress. When they add that with the red shirt in your closet missing a piece of fabric that was found in Leo's hand…"

"So what?"

"So the police are getting ready to—"

The sound of heavy footsteps made me look toward the door and bolt into hiding.

"Miss Bent." Detective Rogers was at the door. "Are you dressed yet? We'd like you to answer a few more questions at the station."

Olivia emerged from the bathroom. "Oh, no thanks, I'd rather answer them here."

The detective's expression showed exactly nothing. "I think we need a change of scene if we're going to get down to the truth."

Olivia scowled. "What truth? I already told that policeman the truth. Leo was a jerk and a perv, but I'd never kill anyone."

"If you'll just come with us, miss, we just want to find out a little more about this Leo. Our folks need to process the rest of the house."

"What about my friends? You're not going to make them come down to the station, too, are you?" Olivia pouted. "This is so embarrassing."

It was such a rich girl thing to say, I wanted to shake her, but her next sentence made me want to slap her, too.

"And that stupid shirt isn't mine, anyway." She

stepped into the hall.

"What shirt is that?" the detective asked.

The realization of her gaffe washed over her face. "Why, that piece of a shirt in Leo's hand, of course."

"Of course," the detective said, and I knew she didn't mean "of course," she meant, "you messed up."

I watched the way Olivia strolled down the hall, her shoulders back but her fingers shaking, and how the detective took her elbow to guide her, strong fingers holding her arm. It was barely a breath's worth of action, but it said everything.

The girls were all going to the police station, leaving me and Em with the police crew. I crawled back up to the ceiling.

"Em?" I tried to call softly, to keep the humans from hearing.

A white spectre appeared in the gloom and moved toward me. The ghost's features became clear as he grew closer—the pink nose and red eyes could only be Em.

"What happened?" he asked.

"The police took all the girls away." I sat back on my haunches. "What do we do now?"

He twitched his nose and ran a paw across his whiskers. "We're mice. I guess we do mice stuff."

"Not mice stuff," I said. "I mean about the

murder. The police think Olivia killed Leo, but we know that's not true."

"So?"

I frowned. "So, we can't just let Olivia go to jail for something she didn't do. It's not right."

"Why do you care what happens to these humans?" He slumped, looking down at the beam he sat upon. "When were they ever kind to us?"

I looked at him sitting there and saw his sadness. "They did bad things to you, didn't they?"

He nodded. "Needles in my back. Fluids in my eyes. Once I was blinded for a long time. My left eye still isn't right."

"I'm sorry." I rubbed against him. "Those people were evil."

We sat like that, watching the gloominess of the attic space turn darker as the afternoon stretched again into evening. I considered his words. People were bad. Olivia was a brat. Why should I care about what happens to her, or any human?

"Because it's not right," I said. My voice was loud enough to fill the space. "The wrong person is being held responsible for something they didn't do."

I was aware of an extreme silence in the house, as the sounds of a clicking camera and general rustling of cabinets stopped.

"I'm sorry, did you say something?" A woman's

voice asked. I thought it sounded like Detective Smythe.

"What?" Officer Alvarez answered. "I thought you said it."

"Me? No. Sounded like someone saying it wasn't right."

"I dunno," he said. "Probably the neighbors."

"Probably."

The undercurrent of shuffling and clicking noises resumed.

I tapped Em on the shoulder and whispered, "Come on, let's go to Leo's attic room."

"Why?"

"We've been through the girls' rooms, focusing on that shirt. Maybe we should see what Leo was hiding." I nodded toward the garage and scampered away.

The second tour of Leo's crawlspace was twice as depressing, even for a mouse. The mattress was old and gray, so thin it could not have been comfortable for a human to sleep on. There were so many lumps and divots, it was like crossing a mountain range for me to walk across. Food wrappers were tossed in every corner.

A rustling of paper in the far corner made me look. Two bright eyes stared at me.

"Em, what are you—?"

A large rat pushed his way from the space, his teeth glowing as he growled at me.

"Oh, excuse me, you're not Em!" I stepped back, preparing to flee.

The rat grasped a half-eaten fry and squeaked.

I wasn't fluent in rat, but I understood. "I don't want your stupid food. It's cold and nasty."

He sat and nibbled on his prize. I stood, waiting to see what he might do. As he kept eating, I decided to continue my search. I moved down the mattress, intrigued by a slip of paper sticking out from underneath.

Little paws are not designed to pull papers out from under heavy human things. I tugged and yanked and huffed to get the paper unstuck. It was almost free when I felt a presence behind me. I turned to see the rat sneaking up, his ears back and teeth bared.

"Squeeeee!" I screamed and ran toward the exit, big rat chasing, grabbing at my tail as I switched it back and forth away from his paws.

I was almost at the wall crack when a whoosh of air and energy stopped me as the rat leapt over me and blocked my escape. He growled again, even meaner this time, but in mid-grrr, he squealed and jumped, holding his bloodied tail. Em stood behind him, his teeth bared.

"Hazel, let's get out of here!" he shouted.

I took two steps and stopped. The rat had retreated to the corner where he sat, licking his wound and studying us. He would not sit there long. I looked over at the papers I'd dropped.

"What are you doing?" Em asked. "Let's go!"

TWELVE

I STARED at him for a moment, then turned and dashed for the papers. Grabbing them in my teeth, I skipped sideways to the crevice, watching the rat who had stopped licking and was now growling again.

"Hurry!" Em stood on guard by the exit, twitching his nose and whipping his tail.

I got to the crack and realized the papers wouldn't fit, at least as flat as they were. Backing through the slot, I grabbed the corner and pulled, folding and crinkling them as they crumpled into the small space and uncrumpled on the other side. They were almost free when I felt a massive push from the other side and heard a squeal. Dropping the papers, I ran to the crack and saw Em trying to get in.

"He's got me!"

I squeezed past him to the rat, whose teeth were into Em's tail up to the gum line as he pulled my friend backward. Enraged, I leapt upon the rat's head and bit down on his ear. He screamed, dropping Em.

"Run!" I shouted as I grabbed the rat's fur and held on. The rat bounded around the room, shaking his head and bucking his body. I kept biting his ear, head, whatever my teeth could sink into while I was being tossed up and down on this rodeo ride.

I was growing dizzy and disoriented. Out of the corner of my eye, I saw the crack in the wall. Giving him one last chomp, I pushed off his head toward my escape and scurried through the crack, pulling my tail up and out of harm's way. As I ran across the beam into the ceiling, I could hear his squeak and growl.

"Pick on someone your own size," I shouted as I ran toward Em.

He was sitting on a beam, holding his bleeding tail. I scurried over and studied his wound.

"Wow, he really bit all the way through, huh?" I said.

"It hurts." He frowned. "Were those papers worth it?"

"I don't know. I'm sorry."

"Can you even read what's on them?"

I shrugged. "I can make out some words."

He pointed, still frowning. "They're over there."

"Yeah, I can look at them in a minute—" I moved to touch his tail.

"No, now." He pulled his tail away from me. "Make my tail chomp worth your need to save useless human papers."

I walked to the wrinkled papers, dejected. Em had not shown this level of annoyance with me, not even when I accidentally almost drowned him. The papers were curled, folded, and somewhat torn. I smoothed them down, walking to the top as I did.

As a baby mouse, I had seen humans look at the squiggles on paper and talk. It didn't take me long to figure out that each set of squiggles meant a different word. I still didn't recognize all the squiggles, but I could read a few words. "Goodnight Moon" was my favorite book.

These papers were filled with big words and numbers. I sat back and cleaned my whiskers.

"So?" Em asked. "Was it worth it?"

"I said I was sorry." I went back over to him. "How bad is your tail?"

"It stings," he said, giving it a lick.

"I wish I could say I knew what was on those papers, but I can't read them. Do you read?"

"Only words from the lab."

I twitched my nose. "Want to see if you know what it says?"

He gave me a look I can only describe as disdainful and walked over to the papers. His paws moved across the paper slowly.

"I don't recognize a lot of these words," he said, "but this word is 'methamphetamine.'"

"Metham…?"

"It's a drug. It made Cue-Three-Oh-Two run around his cage and jump around and shake." He hung his head. "And then he died."

"I am sorry." I nuzzled his shoulder. "Wonder why Leo had these papers."

Voices interrupted us and I skittered to the kitchen ceiling over their source.

"How much longer will you be?" Detective Smythe asked.

"I'm just finishing up," Jerry said. "Nothing earth-shattering so far."

I had an idea. Dragging the topmost paper across the rafters, I stuffed it down the hole next to the overhead light. "You want earth-shattering?" I peered through the hole as the paper sailed to the kitchen table.

"What's that?" The detective pointed.

Jerry picked it up in his gloved hand. "I don't know. It looks like a list. Methamphetamine, 10 units…received? Cocaine, 15…? Here, what do you make of it?"

I heard the snap of a latex glove and spied Smythe taking the paper from him. "If I'm not mistaken, the drug unit was chasing a shipment of meth and coke. How did this get here?"

"It wasn't here before," he said. "I've been sitting here for at least an hour cataloging everything and haven't seen it on the table."

My first idea generated another. Taking another of the papers, I crumpled it as much as possible and ran back to the overhead light. Shimmying down to the bowl, I put the paper in my teeth, took a deep breath and jumped.

To say the two police officers were surprised would be putting it mildly. Jerry gasped. Smythe took a step back and put her hand on her gun. I knew I had very little time to make them understand.

I leapt to the floor, paper still in my mouth and ran to the door. Stopping, I turned and looked at the detective. She stepped toward me, so I moved out of the kitchen. As long as she kept coming, I kept moving. When she stopped, I stopped. Jerry was behind her, his mouth open in disbelief.

"I can't believe I'm following a mouse," Smythe said.

"I can't believe I'm following a detective following a mouse," Jerry replied.

On I led them, down the hall to the door that led to the garage. It was closed, so I stood and scratched at the door, the paper still in my mouth.

"Should we try to get that paper?" Jerry asked.

Smythe shook her head. "I think we should open the door."

I scratched more. My heart had a rapid beat anyway, being a mouse, but at the moment it was positively vibrating. I was cornered. These people could end me with one swift kick.

The detective reached out and turned the knob. I dashed out, then turned and waited. They followed. In the far corner, I climbed the wall to a rope that hung from the ceiling. With one more enormous leap, I grabbed the rope and swung from it. My little nothingness was not heavy enough to pull the trap door open and reveal Leo's hiding space. So I looked at the detective and dropped the paper at her feet.

Jerry reached up to the rope and pulled. Leo's ladder unfolded and I breathed a hefty sigh.

"More orders." The detective held the paper and frowned. "This one has names, although I'll bet they're aliases."

"Let's see what's at the end of this ladder." Jerry nodded upward.

Happy to finally point the two officers in the right direction, I crawled back up to the ceiling and went to find Em. He hadn't moved from his spot on the beam over the kitchen, still licking his poor tail.

"Is the licking helping?" I asked.

"No, it's making it worse," he said between licks. "It will probably get infected and kill me."

"Then why are you doing it?"

"Because at the moment it feels good. And I'm not sure I care if I die."

"Oh, Em." I nuzzled him gently. "I care. Besides, it's not like we live a long time anyway."

"I do." His whiskers drooped. "I was—altered, like, inside my body. They wanted us mice to live longer so they could test things out on us as we got older."

"How much older?"

He shrugged. "I don't know. But maybe we should find a place for me to wash this bite."

We wandered across the beams and slid down to the bathroom. Em crawled over to the sink and stood atop the faucet. He jiggled the handle until the faucet produced a small, steady drip, and climbed down into the sink to catch the drips on his tail.

"See if you can open the drawers and find anti-septic," he said.

"Anti-what?"

"It cleans wounds. They used it in the lab." He sighed. "Can you read anything?"

"A little." My gift allowed mainly for speech and understanding, but I'd learned a little of the human alphabet. "What letters are in it?"

"It might start with an A," he told me. "Or possibly an N."

I scurried to the cabinet under the counter and flattened my body to slip into a crack in the drawer. It was dark, which usually did not bother me, but I found I could not read any of the boxes. Popping halfway out of the crack, I pushed hard against the counter. The drawer budged just enough for me to squeeze my entire body and use my back legs to push against the cabinet while my front legs shoved the drawer. I was rewarded with a good open space to let in light, and to drag out whatever box had the right letter.

The boxes were thrown about, along with toothbrushes, hair ties, and a pink razor. I looked at the first box—it started with a B. I moved that aside and went to the second. It had an I, which was also not correct. I got lucky with the fourth box.

"I found one with an N," I shouted to Em. "N-E-O-S—"

"Neosporin. That's it. Bring it to the front of the drawer. I'll come to it."

I turned to push the box toward the light and saw something large bulging down from underside of the counter. Jumping away with a squeal, I stood quietly until I could make sense of what it was.

"Where did you go?" Em was in the drawer, peering into the darkness.

"I'm here." I took a deep breath and pushed the box into the light. "There's a bag on the ceiling in here."

Em nosed his way into the box and pulled out a slim plastic tube, which he proceeded to chew open and squeeze. Thick white paste bubbled out of the square. He rubbed some onto his front paw, then rubbed the paste on his wound.

"Ow, ow," he squeaked. At last, he stopped and rubbed his paws along his fur. "There. That's better. Now what about the bag?"

I pointed to the roof of the drawer. The large bag I saw was really two smaller bags, taped together to the top of the drawer. I pushed at them both. One was very soft, filled with a powder. The other held rigid objects and resisted my paw.

"What is this?" I asked.

Em joined me and pushed at the hard objects, feeling them with both front paws. "These are syringes...with needles attached. Although—" He felt the softer bag. "This is powder. There are a few drugs you can mix in water and inject, but I think they're all illegal."

I rocked back on my haunches. "How do you know all this?"

"You learn a lot of stuff in a lab. Legal drugs, illegal drugs. How they give the drugs. I didn't so much mind when they mixed it with my food, but they rarely did that. Usually, a big hand would reach in and grab my neck, lift me out of the cage, and poke me with a needle. When they injected Cue-Three-Oh-Two, they gave him one shot then recorded how much he twitched, how many days he stayed awake, what he ate, if anything. Then they gave him other stuff and recorded whether he twitched more or less." He shook his head. "I told you, they did stuff to us."

"That sounds awful." I studied the bags. "I wonder if we could let the police know about this bag. It might be important."

"I'm sure I don't care," Em said. "And I don't know why you want to talk to humans anymore. They only ever try to hurt us."

"That's what I thought, too." I recalled my conversation with Ashley. "And I still think that, mostly. But I wanted a vacation, and all this murder and these police are spoiling my fun, and worse."

"Worse?"

I looked at him. "I told my dad I'd come back. If Olivia gets stuck in jail, I won't be able to. And if I decide to leave this place and go find another spot on this beach, I may never even want to go home."

"It must be nice to have a family waiting for you."

"You said you were all released from the lab at the same time. Why didn't you all stick together?"

"Because there was no 'all' of us to stick. Mom was breeding stock—she had lots of pinkies before she died, so many I cannot remember. The only one I ever knew was my brother. He was Cue-Three-Oh-Two."

"The one they injected with meth?"

Em nodded.

"I'm so sorry." I rubbed my muzzle. "How about we help the police solve this and you can come to my house to live?"

"But what if that girl is the one who did it? What if we can't get to your house?"

I huffed at his question. "Don't be silly, we already know Olivia didn't do it. And if we can't get back to my house, we'll just be a mouse family here on the beach."

As I said that, I realized I was making Em a pretty big promise. Did I want to spend the rest of my life with him?

"Now, let's find a way for the police to find these

bags." I committed myself to finding the real killer. If I was getting stuck with Em, it needed to be at my house, where I had plenty of family to offload him if necessary.

Hugging the baseboards, I scampered down the hall to the kitchen. Detective Smythe was standing at the doorway, still in the garage. She was beating the dust and cobwebs from her crisp gray slacks before entering the house. I stopped at the table, trying to think of a plan.

"That place was equal parts depressing and creepy." Jerry strode from the ladder, holding a phone. "But look what I found."

"I thought they found a phone on the body," Smythe said, opening the door for him.

"They did." He smiled as he set it on the table. "So what's this one for?"

"Burner?" She pressed one of the phone's buttons with her gloved hand. The display lit, showing a gray background and little else. No icons, no apps, just the time and the carrier. "T-Mobile. Maybe we call for account info?"

"We can try. Sometimes they want a subpoena."

She shrugged and went into the hall. "It's a no until you ask."

Jerry continued the task of labeling a bag and storing the phone away as evidence. I watched him and wondered how to get him and the detective into the bathroom. They followed me once. *Maybe I can get him to do it again.*

After watching a few minutes, I saw Jerry put his pen down on the table. I scurried up the table leg, launched myself to the top, and ran for the pen.

"Hey!" He reached for me and stopped. "Don't bite me, buddy, just drop the pen."

"I'm not your buddy," I mumbled through the pen held in my teeth and jumped down, running from the room.

Two sputtering police officers ran after me. I scampered to the bathroom, up the beveled edges of the cabinet, until I balanced myself along the rim of the drawer. Dropping the pen into the drawer, I lifted my nose and stared pointedly at their faces. Smythe had rounded the corner first.

"We already checked the drawers," She said, rubbing her temples. "And why am I talking to vermin?"

"Vermin?" I spat the word, not caring whether she heard me or not. "Why do I want to help you solve this crime when you stupid humans call me names and try to kill me?"

Smythe backed a step until her back hit the door-frame, after which she sank down to her haunches and looked up at me. "Am I losing my mind? How is this possible?"

I sighed. "My story is too long to repeat at the moment. All you need to know is that we saw what happened. It was a woman, but not Olivia. It was dark and we didn't see her face. But there are baggies of powder and needles taped to the upper side of this drawer that might help you."

Jerry's mouth was still hanging open, but he appeared to be listening. The detective stared at me, blinking. Slowly, she rose to her feet.

"Who's we?" she asked.

"A mouse friend of mine." I moved to the cabinet's countertop, away from the drawer.

She stepped forward, keeping her eyes on me the entire time as she reached into the drawer, her palm upward, fingers probing. A light of discovery settled in her eyes. I heard the sound of tape being pulled away and she extracted two baggies.

"Could be coke," she said, rolling the bag of powder around in her hands. "Wonder whose it is."

"There might be fingerprints on the syringes," I said. When she looked at me with a frown, I shrugged. "Sometimes I watch your TV. Olivia likes true crime shows."

She looked at the bag with the syringes. "Prints..." she muttered. "Yeah..." Looking at the

CSU officer, she raised her eyebrows and held out the bags.

Jerry took the bags and walked back toward the great room where he'd left his kit. "I'll bag these and add them to the list."

Smythe nodded. "You okay to draft the warrant for the cell?" She turned toward the cabinet, where I'd flattened myself in a corner, watching. "I need to check one more thing here, and I'll meet you at the station."

"Will do," he said over his shoulder.

The detective turned to the cabinet. "Okay, mouse, where are you?"

THIRTEEN

I STEPPED out of the corner, ready to bolt, and faced her.

"First of all, I'm sorry I called you vermin," she said. "It was uncalled for, although can you really blame me? Mice kind of ruin things for people. You chew up wires, get into our food, and your poop makes us sick."

I stretched myself tall and rigid, ready to fight. "We need to live, too, Detective. Circle of life and all that, you know."

"But we actually work for our—you know what? Never mind. What did you and your little mouse friend see when Leo Carter was being murdered?"

"Well, first of all, that man wasn't very nice," I said as I proceeded to tell her all I knew, beginning with the cameras in the walls and ending with the shadows of two people struggling.

She nodded and wrote as I talked. When I had finished, I sank to all fours and curled my tail around me, spent. I had existed for years without talking to humans, and with no plans to start. And yet, here I was, not only talking to Olivia and Ashley, but spilling everything to this detective. I felt like I had no brain cells left.

"Yeah, those cameras," Smythe said after a moment. "Nothin' but creepy."

"I am sorry that neither my friend nor I could see who it was in the shadows." I ran each paw down my whiskers, one side of my muzzle at a time. "But it did look like self-defense."

"Why wouldn't the woman come forward?"

"Would you?"

There was some silence between us as Smythe turned toward the bathroom mirror. We both gazed at her large brown eyes, set in an angular ebony face. Her shiny black hair was slicked back into a low bun.

"Not as a civilian," she said. "But these girls are the privileged set. They could have killed him in cold blood and their daddies have deep enough pockets to get them off."

I wiggled my nose. "I don't know too much about

those things. Anyway, it doesn't really matter if we saw who did it or not. How would you prove it?"

"Well, you saw what happened, so—" she stopped, frowning.

"So, what? Do you think anyone would believe that your eyewitness is a mouse?"

"They will when you tell them."

"Absolutely not," I said. "It has taken me every ounce of energy to talk to you. I've told you how reluctant I am to deal with humans. You and Ashley are bad enough, and I swore I'd never talk to Olivia. After this, I'm done with the lot of you."

I hopped down from the counter and ran off, mad at her, mad at all humans, and most of all, mad at myself. Slipping into a crack in the wall I wondered where Em had hidden himself. I wanted to call out to him, but I didn't want the detective to hear me.

"Why don't you speak mouse?" I muttered in a soft growl.

"No one taught me."

I jumped at the voice behind me. Em sat in a corner of the wall, pressed against a wooden support.

"Em," I whispered, "I was looking for you."

"Why are you whispering?" He spoke in a normal tone.

"Shh. I don't want the humans to hear us." I saw

a crack in the opposite side of the drywall, a small slit that emitted a shard of light. "Let's get out of here."

I scampered toward the daylight and emerged on the side of the house, next to the outdoor faucet. Looking back, I saw Em had joined me.

"Are we going to have more fun?" he asked.

"No." I nodded toward the beach. "We're going to find another house to live in, hopefully one without dead bodies."

The house to the left of Olivia's place seemed unoccupied. It was a smaller place, with blue paint chipping and peeling from the boards. Its porch was barely worth the name, being a few pieces of wood nailed together and resting on the sand. The front door was not a proper door at all, but a sliding glass one.

I pounced onto the porch, preparing to slip in and check it out. As I ran past the sliding glass door, I heard a growl and looked to my right. A gigantic terrier leapt at the glass, his teeth gleaming in the sunlight. My quick heartbeat went from a vibration to a steady hum and I half-scampered, half-fell into the sand and away from the monster.

"Okay," I whispered as I caught my breath. "Not there."

Em looked even paler than usual, which looked odd enough for an albino mouse.

"Are you alright?" I asked.

He nodded and fidgeted with his whiskers. "You scared me. I confess, I feel lost without you."

I gave him my best mousey smile. "The good thing about not growing up in a lab is that I've learned a thing or two about strange places and things that want to eat you."

We scampered through the sand to the next house. It had a raised porch with a proper red wooden door and a large window in the middle of it. As we reached the steps, the door opened and a young woman came out, followed by a man of a similar age. Em and I dove under the steps.

"What are we gonna do?" The man asked. "Leo was our dealer."

"Relax," the woman told him. "We can work with his associate."

"Do you know his associate?"

Em nuzzled me to move away from the steps, but I shook my head.

"They're talking about Leo," I whispered. "I want to listen."

He frowned and sat back on his haunches, nervously picking at his fur.

"She stays in the background," the woman was saying, "but I know who she is."

"With all the police activity, will she still be in

business?" The man sounded skeptical. "I mean, especially his murder. They're probably going to find out what he was up to."

"Possibly, but they'll have to tie her to his drug supply first. And even if they do, she's got a hot-shot criminal lawyer for a dad, so she won't be doing any time for it."

The man's footsteps clomped down the stairs, rattling the step we hid under. "I don't care about her. I care about my weekly score."

I watched them wander down the beach toward the pier. No doubt they would meet friends, have some drinks, and not think about giving the cops any tips that would solve Leo's murder.

Why should they? "Why should anyone?" I said in an angry voice.

"Why should anyone what?" Em asked.

"Sorry." I nodded toward the couple. "They could tell the police what they know and solve this murder in two shakes of a rat's tail. But they won't because they don't want to get in trouble and don't want to give up their drugs."

"And we don't want to either now, right? Because?"

"Because I finally remember I don't like humans and I don't want to get involved in their hijinks." I looked at him. "You were right. They've done nothing but try to trap us, kill us, or use us for—bad reasons. Why do I care who murders who?"

Em's whiskers drooped. "I know all about the bad reasons. Does this mean we stay here instead of going home to your family?"

My family. I stepped from the shadows and hung my head. "I guess I'm beginning to doubt if I'll be going home. If Olivia is charged with murder, she'll never go home again. And if her luggage doesn't go back to Riverside, neither will I—or you."

"What are we gonna do?"

I looked out at the beach and the ocean beyond. From where we sat, the rise of land hid the shoreline, but I could see the waves rising, rising, then cresting as they raced to their finish line. The air smelled salty and sour at the same time, dense even in the brightness of the day. A breeze tickled the palm trees and ruffled my fur. It was a beautiful place, a place I knew as home. I could stay here forever.

But I couldn't leave my family—not if I could help it.

FOURTEEN

"WE'RE GOING to go back into that house," I said with a resigned sigh. "I'm going to cooperate with the detective so we can get Olivia back to her home, and we can go with her."

"But, other than the drugs, what do we know?"

I nuzzled him to turn around. "We know who killed Leo," I said, and dashed back toward our beach house.

As we scampered, I could hear Em trying to ask me questions, but he couldn't run and talk at the same time, so all I got were occasional syllables.

"How…(puff)…do…(huff)…WE knOW…" his voice bounced with every step.

I stayed quiet until we got to our patio door, still open while the police completed their tasks. Jerry stepped out as we slipped in. I noted that he was taking off gloves and unbuttoning his coveralls.

"I'm almost done here," he told someone on the phone. "If you could pick up Miles I'll be home to fix dinner in about half an hour. Thanks, Hon."

Family business, I thought. *Even humans want to get home.*

I ran ahead of Em. "I'll look in Olivia's room," I told him. "You look in the bathroom."

"For what?"

"For Detective Smythe." My reply was a bit snappish. "Sorry, I thought you knew."

He gave me a mousey smile, but on him only one lip curved upward. I wasn't certain if it was because humans had done something to his face, or he just never smiled before. I smiled back and headed toward the bedroom.

The room was empty and dark. I sat very still and listened. Soon I heard the staccato steps of a precise woman. Detective Smythe was in the hallway.

"Detective!" I yelled as I ran toward her. "Detective, I have news!"

I don't blame her for not hearing me. She was not expecting to see me, and my little mouse voice did not exactly ring out in the space. Her rubber soles squeaked on the wood floor, headed right toward me. To avoid my fate of being stepped on, I backed up, ran to the side, then hopped on her foot.

To say it was a wild ride would be an understatement. Her leg propelled the foot forward, allowing the sturdy black shoe to rise comically in the air, then plop down again as if it were only vaguely attached to the leg. I could not hang onto this rollercoaster. Grabbing her shoelace, I swung up to her pant leg and proceeded to crawl up the front of her.

"Detective Smythe!" I shouted as I climbed up her pants to her shirt.

"Aaagh-ugh-urgle," she screamed as she ran backward, trying to shake me off.

At least the rollercoaster of her shoe had a steady rhythm to it. Now I was being violently tossed up, down, and sideways while my claws clung to the buttons on her shirt. She kept backing up as she made sounds that did not even approximate words. I held on, not wanting to fall to the tile floor.

"Detective." I called to her again, my voice warbling in the action. "It's me. I have news."

I felt her body falling away and I squealed. She had managed to back through the kitchen door, and I saw the table within reach, so I jumped. Smythe landed with a thud in a chair, rocking onto the back legs before righting herself. My front paws hit the table's edge, but I was able to scramble up with my back legs and flopped on my belly, catching my breath.

Smythe looked down at me, her chest heaving. "Don't ever do that again."

"Sorry," I exhaled, my own ribs trying to keep up with my lungs. Panting, I told her, "I think I know who killed Leo."

She sat upright and put both forearms on the table, one on each side of me. "Who is it?"

I relayed the beach couple's conversation. "I've only heard one girl in this house talk about her dad being an attorney—Brina. Olivia's dad is a doctor. Brina said her dad is a criminal lawyer."

"Do you know what the others' dads do?"

"No," I admitted. "I suppose you should find out for certain."

Smythe took out her phone and stared at it. "How am I supposed to tell Detective Rogers that I got my intel from a mouse?"

I shrugged. "You could say you overheard the conversation."

"Oh, no." She frowned. "That's all kinds of trouble. I can't go into a court and commit perjury."

"I suppose." I sat back on my haunches, wishing for something to nibble. "And I'm certainly not taking the stand."

We fell silent, lost in our whirling minds.

Smythe broke the stillness. "Well at least we have Carter's laptop and phone. We can point our investigation towards the specific gal."

"It may take a while," I mused, as Officer Alvarez stepped into the hall.

"When does our relief arrive?" he asked.

Smythe looked at her phone. "Rogers just texted me. Girls have been processed. They're being released on their own recognizance."

I could see the young officer nod and pull out a phone. By human standards, he was young, fresh-faced. I waited until he was in the other room.

"How old is Officer Alvarez?" I asked.

"He's pretty new. Twenty-three, I think."

"If he was wearing different clothes, he'd blend right in with the beach crowd," I said. "Like, he could probably talk to people, and they'd talk to him..."

"Undercover." Smythe looked down the hall. "That's what you're talking about."

"I bet a young human looking for drugs might find out who supplies them in this neighborhood."

The detective shook her head. "It'd be dicey. They might not want to trust a stranger."

"He wouldn't be a stranger if Olivia introduced him as her cousin," I said.

"How do we know Olivia isn't working with Leo,

too? Just because one of her friends is, doesn't mean the rest of them aren't."

I cleaned my whiskers. She was right. "Okay…are there any houses here that the police could rent?"

"That's going to take too long." She sighed. "Plus, getting permission from the department to put him in undercover, planning all the logistics, we should keep working on the tech end of the case."

"Are you talking to someone in here?" Officer Alvarez wandered into the room. "I keep hearing voices—and not the crazy kind."

I froze. It was instinct to keep very still and hope the predator didn't see me.

He looked straight at me. "Look, a mouse. Kinda cute."

For a moment, I lost any ability to move. A human called me 'cute.' I lifted my nose and wiggled it, attempting to sniff as much as I could. He smelled like lemons and mint, and perhaps a little eucalyptus, and he smiled at me as he reached his hand toward the counter where I sat. It was such a slow gesture that I sat and watched it for much longer than I should have. By the time he put his palm flat on the cool quartz, I was hypnotized.

I placed one paw on his thumb, still watching for any quick movements. He held perfectly still as I climbed upon his knuckles. *What am I doing?* My sense of survival returned to me, and I turned to jump off. He let me go.

"Were you talking to the mouse?" he asked the detective.

"Yeah, yeah, just talking to myself, you know." She tried to sound confident, but I could hear the anxiety in her voice "And the mouse, as long as he was there."

I forgot myself completely. "She," I blurted before placing my front paws over my mouth.

Alvarez's smile took over his face. "Oh. My. God you can talk?"

I looked at Smythe, who said, "Might as well. Cat's out of the bag now if you'll pardon the expression."

Alvarez looked at me, happy expectation in his eyes.

"Hello," I said. "My name is Hazel."

"Nice to meet you, Hazel," he said. "My name is Tom."

"Tom, Detective Smythe and I were talking about how she could prove what I've already told him. I know who killed Leo Carter."

"Great, you can tell us!"

Smythe shook her head. "How would that go? 'Hey, Captain, a mouse overheard a conversation and knows who killed Carter.'"

He grimaced. "Right. That does sound like all kinds of crazy."

"And really, you don't know that the girl killed him," Smythe said. "You just know she's his assistant in the drug business."

I shrugged. "True. We need to talk to people, but they need to talk back to us."

"Us?" Alvarez laughed. "Should I get you a tiny badge?"

I did not laugh. "I could use a tiny gun right now."

"Ooh, sarcasm from vermin," Smythe said. "I'm impressed."

"I told you not to call me that." I bared my teeth.

"Sorry," she said. "I'm frustrated and I shouldn't take it out on you."

"You know, there is also the matter of the blouse," I told her.

"Yeah, we found that in Olivia's room."

"But it was put there by someone else. Look at Olivia's room—it's neat, organized. She has a place for her laundry. Why would she crumple a shirt in the corner?"

Smythe nodded. "Carter had the tab from that blouse in his hand, so whoever he was fighting is the one who killed him."

"Still circumstantial." Alvarez shrugged. "How are we going to figure out who was wearing it?"

"Rayon," a tiny voice squeaked from the far corner.

Detective Smythe looked over and saw Em flattened between the toilet and the tub. "Another one?"

"I told you I have a friend," I said.

After the woman finished shaking her head and blowing air from her mouth, she sighed one more enormous sigh and asked, "Well, what's this about rayon?"

Em gazed up at me.

"You mentioned it," I told him. "You explain it."

One slow step at a time, Em moved away from the corner. "Humans wear the same kind of fabric. The blouse is made of rayon, really old rayon. It belongs to someone who wears old clothes."

"So, vintage?" Smythe asked. "Does Brina wear vintage clothes?"

I looked at Em for an answer.

"Her clothes were all new," he said. "Silks, linens, high quality, very tasty."

The two humans stared at him.

"I was a lab mouse," he said, standing rather proudly. "I ate napkins."

"We need to identify Brina as the drug dealer." I stood on my back legs and wiggled my whiskers.

"We?" Smythe smiled. "Are we back to needing the tiny badge and gun?"

I sank back down on all fours. "You, then. I should have just kept my mouth shut and my knowledge to myself." I turned to Em. "Maybe we find our own way back to Riverside."

The detective knelt by the counter until we were facing one another. "I am grateful for the information. We hardly ever get firsthand accounts. But you know as well as us how awkward this all is. Don't worry, we'll figure out a way to draw this Brina out."

"Wait." Em had ventured to the middle of the small room. "Brina may be the drug dealer, but the blouse is not hers."

"He's right." I cleaned my whiskers. "We checked the rooms. There's a pair of shorts in Claire's things —they match the shirt."

Smythe exchanged glances with Alvarez before jerking her head toward the hall. "Claire's room is second to the right."

The officer left the room, and I felt a tug on my leg.

"I'm hungry," Em said.

"I don't think they left the cheese out, but there's granola in the pantry," I told him, and turned to Smythe. "We've helped enough. You should be able to take it from here."

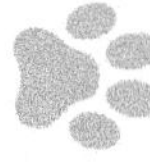

FIFTEEN

IN THE KITCHEN, Em and I were up to our ears in granola and chocolate-covered nuts when I heard the detective say, "I think she's the one."

I heard Alvarez's footsteps into the kitchen as he spoke. "I found the shorts. I'm no fashion judge, but they seem to go with that red blouse."

"Claire's?" Smythe asked.

"Yep."

Stuffing one more nut into my cheek, I ran forward to the edge of the cupboard door and looked out.

"Whrrugoon?" Em burbled as he chewed.

"Shh, I want to hear."

"So then, Claire is our killer?" Alvarez asked.

"Not necessarily." Smythe shook her head as she took her phone out and pushed some buttons. "Girls do borrow each other's clothes. But it places reasonable doubt…Ronda? We found more stuff at the house. I can fill you in…Yes, we can have the place cleared within the hour…Okay."

"What's up?" Alvarez asked.

"Rogers says she's bringing the girls back."

"So Olivia is off the hook?" Alvarez asked.

"No and neither are we." Smythe grinned. "Rogers and I are going to stick around and monitor the girls' movements, at least until the surveillance team gets here."

A surveillance team? I pushed the cupboard door open. It swung easier than I thought, and I clung to the bottom of the wood as it swayed out, past the countertop.

"Detective," I yelped. "I have an idea."

I felt fabric under my back paws and let go of the cabinet. Alvarez was holding a dishtowel up for me to fall onto, after which he deposited me onto the counter.

"Thank you. Perhaps you could ask the surveillance unit to pay special attention to Brina's whereabouts? You might find out if she's dealing drugs."

"True, but what's my reasoning? I can't really tell them a mouse gave me the scoop."

I sighed. "Just tell them you've got a feeling about

her. How do you say it? That 'you had a hunch.' I mean, you did find those drugs in the bathroom."

The detective stood near the couch, a red piece of fabric in her hands. Alvarez looked at her. She shrugged.

"I'll do it if you don't want to," she said. "What will it hurt?"

"Nah." Alvarez shook his head. "You claim the shorts, I'll talk to surveillance. We'll both either share the collar or the blame."

By nightfall, the house was filled again, as the four young women had returned and, after long naps, busied themselves with showers, makeup and general frou-frou as they prepared to go out. Em and I agreed to split up. I'd watch Brina and he'd watch Claire. On my way to Brina's room, I stopped by the eaves over the garage and studied the street.

It was narrow, much narrower than the street in front of my home in Riverside. A normal police car would not be able to park for normal surveillance. How would the police be able to keep an eye on us?

"Bri, have you got a flat iron?" Olivia yelled from her room.

"No, I think Ashley's got one," was her response.

I scampered over to Brina's bedroom and peered in from a crack in the ceiling. Laying on the dresser, atop a hand towel, was a pink flat iron. *Why would she lie?* I was tempted to run to Olivia's room and tattle, but I stopped. Instead, I stayed and watched.

No matter what kind of police surveillance Brina had tonight, I'd be following her every step.

Brina scrutinized her reflection in the mirror over the dresser, turning left and right, using a small sponge to dab at her face. Flipping her straight black hair behind her shoulders, she picked up the flat iron and squeezed the handle, twisting it open.

I leaned forward to see what was inside and saw her pull out a small pink bag, the same color as the flat iron. My left foot slipped down the wall and I half-fell, half-skidded to the floor. Brina gasped and turned toward the door, so I scooted under the bed and looked up at her.

She sighed in relief. "Get a grip, Bri." Putting the pink bag in her black Prada purse and giving her form-fitting dress a tug, she sauntered out the door. I scampered after her, hugging the wall and stopping at corners to hide.

"It's about time," Olivia said from the porch, where she was sitting with Claire, Ashley, and a pitcher of something green. "We've got margaritas."

I crawled into one of the planters and continued to watch the group from under a large red geranium.

"Ohmygod, I need this so much," Ashley said as

she poured another round in her glass. "That was intense."

"I know, right?" Olivia ran her glass across her forehead. "My head's on fire."

Claire leaned forward. "What did they ask you?"

Olivia counted on her fingers. "How long did I know Leo Carter? What did I do yesterday? Can anyone vouch for where I was? Did I hate Leo Carter? Did any of you hate Leo?"

The rest of the women nodded. "Pretty much what they asked me," Ashley said.

"Oh—and they wanted to know if I owned a red blouse." Olivia frowned. "Red's not my color."

I saw Claire's face turn pinker and her eyes twitched once. "I know! Why would they ask that?"

"Probably needed some fashion advice." Brina cocked an eyebrow and reached for her drink. "The guys two doors down invited us to party. Want to go?"

"When did they invite us?" Ashley asked. "We were at the police station all day."

Brina held up her phone. "Don't be a dope. They texted. I told them where we were, they said they'd have pizza and White Claws to help us de-stress."

"Nah." Olivia waved her glass. "Imma stay here. I don't feel like a party."

"Why not? We've only got a day left here." Brina frowned.

Olivia glared at her, and the silence grew uncomfortable, even for a mouse.

"A man was stabbed in my bedroom." Each word was a harsh staccato. "I'm not in the mood."

"Sorry, not sorry." Brina shrugged. "You didn't even like him."

Olivia put her glass on the table, held her face in both hands and sobbed. I'd seen her throw tantrums at home when she didn't get her way, but this was the first time I'd ever witnessed raw emotion from her. My first, odd instinct was to run to her for support, and it struck me how far our relationship had come in just two short days.

"What's wrong?" Em whispered as he climbed into the planter with me.

"Where have you been?"

"Well, I watched Claire like you said, and when she left, I was going to follow, but something caught my eye." He sat down and rubbed his ear.

"So, hurry and tell me," I growled. "I think Brina's going to leave and I'm going to have to chase after her."

"I was watching Claire get ready—if these girls only knew the kinds of chemicals they were putting on their skin—anyway, Claire is putting on mascara, then she pulls a little bag from behind the mirror, looks at it, opens it, sighs, closes it, and puts it back." He wiggled his whiskers. "Then she left. Naturally, I had to see what was in the bag."

"What was it?"

"Some kind of powder. White."

I nodded. "I think probably drugs. Too bad the police officers left. They were supposed to have a surveillance team here, but I haven't seen any cars."

"What should I do now?" he asked.

Brina got up and tugged at her skirt. "Do what you like, I'm going to get my party on."

I turned to Em. "I have to follow Brina. You keep watch over Claire. If those officers come back, do you think you can talk to them?"

"Oh, I don't know…"

"Em, it's important. I can't be here to talk for us. If Alvarez or Boyd show up, they need to know about the drugs in Claire's room."

His ears drooped, and his pink eyes got large. "I'll try, Hazel. But I hope you come back before they do."

Giving him a quick nuzzle, I said, "I have confidence in you. You've been a very brave mouse so far."

SIXTEEN

BRINA HEADED out from the porch, so I scurried after her, trying to run quickly and hide often. Her shoes barely fit the name, flat soles with thin, bejeweled straps, but they were great for striding along the sand to the party house. I could usually outrun any of these girls and found myself running more than I was hiding.

There were still quite a few humans out as the sun was setting. Even the house next door had lights on, with two flaxen-haired surfer guys draped over their chairs. Fortunately, they were not looking for a little gray mouse so I could scamper unobserved. Brina and I reached the neighbor's house at the same time. The music that had been heard at Olivia's house was louder here, coming from the balcony above the front door. It banged about in my little mouse head, and I wished Em had come with me, just for the support.

"Bri!" A man shouted, then ran down the stairs. He grabbed the girl to hug her, but she pushed back.

"Whoa, there, Cassanova. Did you get the money?"

"Almost."

Brina put her hand up and turned away. "Why do I bother with you deadbeats? I'm going to the pier and get some action."

"Hold on, Baby." He gripped her arm and she winced. "I got something better than cash to exchange."

"Ugh, as if." She clawed at his hand, but he held firm. "Knock it off, Tyler."

"Little bird told me the cops are looking for a girl wearing a red blouse last night. Just happens, I got a picture they might like to see." The young man pulled out his phone and I scrambled up the side of the staircase, looking for a place to be able to see over his shoulder.

It was a photo of a sunset, layers of orange and red highlighting the beach in shimmering lines.

Brina had stopped struggling and pointed at the scene. "What does that prove?"

He used his fingers to enlarge a portion. In the right

corner, two blurry figures entered Olivia's house. The person facing the camera was undeniably Leo Carter. The one facing away was wearing a familiar red blouse, oversized on her small frame. Straight black hair hung over the collar and halfway down her back.

"It was Brina!" I said, then clasped both front paws over my mouth.

The two humans looked up at me, their faces squinting in confusion. I dove onto the man's shoulder, and he screamed. Dropping the phone, he began jumping backward, falling down the steps and landing on his butt.

I leapt from the man and ran to the phone perched on the stair. Pushing the phone to the sand below, I jumped down and continued to push the phone away from the action, under the stairway and under a small shrub, where I buried it. Now I just had to get the police to find the evidence before Brina and her male friend got to it.

While I stole the man's phone, he was busy standing and brushing himself off, keeping a running stream of expletives going about the mouse who jumped on him, and looking at the stairs. I believe the term humans use is "freaking out."

"Oh my god a mouse did you see it a mouse it jumped right on me maybe it has rabies or something

I should go to the emergency room and get tested or something what should I do?"

Brina laughed. "What do I care? I hope you get hantavirus."

I nearly shouted my displeasure. How dare she think I spread anything so common?

"Well, at least help me find my phone," he said. "It's getting dark—let me use your phone's flashlight."

"To find the phone with incriminating evidence? Not a chance, Tyler." She turned toward the pier and strolled off, waving her hand lazily.

"You know I'm going to find it eventually," he yelled after her.

"Eventually is a long way away," she called over her shoulder and kept walking.

I wanted to dash after her, but I didn't want this Tyler-fellow finding his phone. It was much too heavy for me to carry, and I had dug the shallowest of holes to bury it. I watched Brina slip further from me and stepped forward to follow her.

A bright light swept in front of me, and I jumped back into the shrubbery. Tyler had found a flashlight and was shining it in all the cracks and nooks. I made myself very flat and small and tried to blend in with the plants. The light washed across me, held steady for a moment, then moved on.

I looked up again, searching for Brina. She had disappeared. I shoved more dirt on top of the phone and left. With any luck, he would decide to wait until morning to find his phone. I could retrieve it later—hopefully with some help from Em.

Avoiding the spotlight, I scampered across the sand toward the pier, looking for signs of Brina's movements. She had said she was going to the pier, and I headed that direction. The sand was deep, and I could not run as quickly as I wanted. Still, I pressed on, finding patches of flat ground where I gained traction, until I saw a familiar form sashaying to the boardwalk.

Tide was out, so I ran through the wet sand and crawled up the pillar to meet Brina at the beginning of the long wooden pier that extended out past the beach, into the waves. A mom-and-pop burger joint sat on the large round end. I remembered our dad sneaking us into their pantry where we'd snack on delicious, sweet buns and chips.

Tonight, there was music thumping from the boardwalk, and young humans fading in and out of bars, strolling out to the burger place and back, red cups full. Brina went into a bar with a pelican on the front. I slipped under the door and flattened myself against the wall. Brina was working her way through the crowd, smiling and flirting with everyone.

As she approached the bar, two familiar-looking guys nodded to her. I recognized them as the surfers in the house next to ours. She gave them a coquettish grin and signaled the bartender, who smiled back and reached for a glass.

A short sweaty man appeared behind her and put his hand around her waist. Still smiling, she turned and removed his hand, but he returned it, tightening his grip. Frowning, she pulled away from him, which made him grasp her arm and drag her toward him. She pushed at his chest, growling a curse.

One of the surfers stood, turned, and grabbed the man by the back of his shirt in such a fluid motion, it was difficult for even my quick brain to process. The short man stood on his tiptoes, being hanged by his shirt collar, while the surfer whispered something in his ear. Whatever it was, it made the short man's eyes widen. The surfer released him, and he staggered into the night.

"Oh my god, thank you," Brina told him. "Are you vacationing here, too?"

"Yeah, name's Joe. I'm from Anaheim." He gestured to his right. "This is my friend, Dane. I think we're in the house next to you and your friends. We rented it for the summer."

So began a conversation that humans like to have and I like to ignore. All about what they like and what they don't, in food and music, et ceter. I don't understand how any being would have an opinion about food. You need food to live. Eat the food.

At some point, I heard one of the surfers say, "I hear our neighbors throw a fine party."

"Depends on how you like it," Brina said. "Cheap booze, Costco snacks, but quality pharmaceuticals."

Dane shook his head, but Joe smiled. "That's what I'm talkin' 'bout."

"Well, then, come with me." Brina ran her hand down his shirt. "We can finish our business on the way to the party."

The trio left the bar. I followed, zigzagging my way between all the feet that were crowding into the space. It was easy to keep a steady distance from them as they walked on, easily recognizable from their silhouettes. Brina kept a steady flow of chatter, leaning against one man, then the other, slapping at them every time she laughed. She reminded me of the ball in a pinball machine.

As we approached the party house, the music grew louder. Brina stopped and turned to Joe.

"Maybe we should settle up here before we go inside," she said. "It's uber-loud in there and I don't want to shout our deal."

Joe nodded and reached in his pocket. "Good idea. How much?"

"One-twenty. It's the good stuff." Brina slid her hand into her small leather purse, looking down to hunt about until she pulled out a small baggie of white powder.

As she and the man exchanged dollars and baggies, Dane reached into his pocket and pulled out strange wallet. He opened it and I saw something shiny—a badge.

"Brina Templeton, you're under arrest for position with the intent to distribute." He grabbed her left hand to place behind her back, but she fought him off.

"As if!" She wheeled to face Joe, who held a pair of white strips.

"Sorry, Bri. I'm Detective Allen and this is my partner Detective Green." He put the strips around her wrists and tightened them. The strips made a zipping noise.

I've heard plenty of angry humans before, but I thought Brina was going to burst into flames. She began with cursing and ended with guttural sounds that did not even attempt to form words. For a few moments, she attempted to kick at the detectives.

"You know, I have zip-ties, too," Detective Allen said. "We can put them on your ankles and carry you out if you wish."

I've never seen a human collect themselves more

quickly than Brina's transformation into a reasonable young woman. She stood still, shook her hair and adjusted her shoulders before glancing at both men and walking between them.

As they led her away, I ran back to our beach house. Brina was now arrested for the drugs, but I needed to get Tyler's phone to the police for proof that she murdered Leo. And I couldn't do that alone.

The house was dark when I arrived. Where could they have all gone? I crept through the rooms, calling softly for Em. He didn't answer. I was happy that he had followed Claire, but still wished to find him.

Loud music interrupted my thoughts, coming from Tyler's party. I supposed that was a place to look for the girls—perhaps they had decided to cheer themselves with a night of dancing and drinking among beach friends. Scampering toward the music, I decided if they weren't there, I'd at least get some food for my empty belly.

SEVENTEEN

ASHLEY WAS the first one I spotted, in a bright white romper, dancing on the balcony, laughing. If she was here, probably the others were, too. I went on the hunt for Claire, hoping to find Em.

The house was much larger than Olivia's, two stories full of young bodies and lots of noise. I stayed close to baseboards and ran in short spurts to avoid attracting notice. Olivia was in the living room, sitting in a dark blue papasan chair. She held a red cup in her hand and looked at the people talking about Harry Styles. I only knew about him because she'd manipulated her dad into VIP tickets to his last concert in L.A. I expected her to be sharing her wild night at the concert with her party friends—I remember she'd come home wearing a t-shirt auto-graphed by him and his band.

Instead, she sat impassively, running her finger around the rim of her cup. She looked so sad to me, I wanted to go comfort her. I was certain my presence would not be welcomed, and I decided to keep looking for Claire.

As I crept through the various rooms, it occurred to me that my feelings toward Olivia had changed significantly. I didn't care for the spoiled and entitled Olivia, but this sober young woman pulled at my mousey heartstrings. As I rounded the corner of the last step to the second floor, I heard Claire's voice.

"It wasn't like that," she said.

I scampered toward the noise and found her with Tyler in one of the bedrooms.

"Look, all I'm saying is that I got photos on my phone, and for the right price, I won't hand them to the cops."

"You don't even have your phone."

He shrugged. "I'll prolly find it in the morning. Even if I don't, all my photos get uploaded to the Cloud."

"You're such a jerk. I don't have money."

He touched her shoulder. "It doesn't have to be cash."

"Eeww." She pushed his hand away. "You know I have a girlfriend."

"Perfect! It can be a threesome."

"Triple ick." She walked toward the door, but Tyler caught her by the arm and turned her toward him.

"I don't care how, but either I get paid or you get arrested."

"Get off of me!" Claire fought to be free of his grasp.

He was strong and held her firmly. As they struggled, I saw white fur run past me to Tyler's leg. Em crawled on the guy's sandal and sank his teeth into his foot. Tyler screamed and leapt in the air. I scurried forward to help Em, as he had been launched upward with the guy's jump. He fell on me, and we rolled in a tangle until we could get to our feet and run under the bed.

"Wow, Em, that was brave," I whispered.

He sat up and cleaned his whiskers. "I don't understand what they were saying, but that human is mean."

I peeked out at the room. Tyler and Claire were gone, so I turned back to Em. "I do understand. I just don't know what to do with it."

Em cocked his head. "What would you have to do?"

I told him about Tyler's phone buried in the

bushes. "I was hoping to get your help moving the phone over to Olivia's so we could get it to the police. But now I'm not certain. Maybe we lose his phone permanently."

"You heard what he said. The photos get uploaded, whether he has the phone or not."

"I heard that, but I don't know what it means."

Em wiggled his nose. "At the lab, the humans were always uploading their photos, then deleting them from their phones. Then they'd look at the pictures on their computers."

"So, basically, the photos are now on Tyler's computer." I sat and ran my paws along my whiskers. "If we get the phone to the police, they'll see whatever photos Claire doesn't want them to see. If we don't, Claire has to decide how much she's willing to give to keep Tyler from handing the photos to them."

"What do we do?"

I sat quietly for a few minutes. "The truth is the truth," I said at last. "Whatever those photos show, the police need to know about it. Come help me."

We scampered back down the stairs and I ran to the bushes, Em on my heels. I hoped the phone was still buried. I also hoped it wasn't.

One hard edge was still visible when we got to

the spot. Em helped me dig the rest of the phone out and we pushed it along the edge of the house toward our place.

"What are we going to do with it once we get it home?" Em asked.

"Somehow, we get it to the police. Maybe the detectives will come back tomorrow."

"Maybe." He didn't sound convinced.

Even with help, pushing and pulling a cell phone was hard work. We had to stop and rest several times before we got it to our porch area. I looked around the outside for a place to hide it. The planters were too tall to lift the phone into, and the patio area was sparsely decorated.

Em pointed to the phone. "I wish we could just call the detective."

"Yes," I said, tapping at the black screen with my paw. "Why couldn't we?"

"Because it's probably locked. At the lab, all the humans locked their phones."

The solution hit me like a bolt of lightning. Using the pad of my paw, I pushed at the screen. It took a lot of pressure, but a photo of a glass of beer finally appeared. "Maybe if we called 9-1-1," I suggested and jumped on the icon at the bottom of the screen.

The phone displayed the number and a green

symbol to indicate it was in use. I heard a faint voice saying, "Nine one one, what's your emergency?"

I spoke louder than I've ever spoken in my life. "I need to speak to Detective Smythe."

"Ma'am, this is an emergency line."

"It is an emergency," I shouted. "It's regarding a murder investigation and I'm being forced to use someone else's phone to call for help!"

It wasn't strictly a lie.

The dispatcher was immediately more helpful. "I'll try to patch you through. What is your name?"

Had I told her my name? I couldn't remember. *I'll give her a clue.* "Hazel Graymouse. It's about the Leo Carter murder."

"Hang on, Ms. Graymouse," she said.

It took a few minutes before I heard a familiar woman's voice on the line. "This couldn't possibly be who I think it is."

"Yes, Detective. I'm calling you from a phone that belongs to a guy named Tyler. He has pictures of the night of Leo's murder. Pictures that will show who was wearing the red shirt."

"Where are you, Hazel?"

"On our patio at the beach house. Please come quickly."

"Now what?" Em asked.

"We wait for the detective."

He said nothing for a moment, then rubbed his cheeks. "I'm hungry."

"Me, too." I looked at the phone. "We shouldn't leave this alone…well, I shouldn't. You could go eat and bring me something?"

"Okay. I'll be right back." He turned and scurried inside.

I hated to see him leave, even if I was hungry. The dark felt suddenly ominous, as if something might reach down and snatch the phone—or me. I flattened myself down on the screen and waited.

I heard voices getting louder. I could distinguish Olivia as one of the group.

"Ohmygod, Brina's been arrested." It sounded like she was crying. "What's happening around here?"

"Brina wasn't very smart." This was Tyler's voice, which scared me. While his phone was behind the planter, it wasn't well hidden, and there's only so much a little mouse can do to defend herself. "Turns out those guys staying next to us were cops—she sold them coke."

"That's crazy," Olivia said. "Brina's no dealer."

"Are you kidding?" Ashley had returned with them. "How did you not know? Brina's been supplying lots of people here."

"Of course, she didn't know." Brina emerged

from the shadows, running and looking over her shoulder. "If the cops ask, you didn't see me."

Olivia gasped. "Bri! What have you gotten into?"

"Shut up, your voice carries for miles around here!" Brina grabbed Olivia by the shoulders. "I'm just gonna grab my stuff and get outta here. I swear if you don't help me I'll never speak to you again."

The phone I was lying on vibrated and a loud, thumping noise came from it. I jumped off, startled.

"Hey," Tyler said, hunting around the patio. "That's my phone. Where is it?"

By this time, Brina was closest to the planter. She reached down and picked the phone up. I ran forward to nip at her but hesitated. I might have been brave earlier, but my natural instinct was still to hide from humans, not run out and bite them.

Tyler rushed toward her. "Give me that. How did it even get here?"

She backed away, holding the phone away from him. "Don't know, don't care. Let me take care of a few photos first."

"Good luck. It's locked."

"Oh, please. Everyone knows your password is 1-1-1-1. It's the only thing you can remember when you're lit." She tapped the screen hard, then used her finger to scroll. "Ah, yes, the photos."

"I might like to see those first." Detective Smythe

walked through the back door, onto the patio. "And I believe some of my precinct friends would like a meeting with you, Ms. Templeton. They are most displeased that you evaded arrest."

Brina threw the phone away from her and turned to run, but the detective caught the device while nodding toward the street. Four uniformed officers appeared and surrounded the dark-haired woman, who tried her best to slip through their grasps. Detective Rogers stepped into the melee and grabbed Brina by her ponytail, yanking her onto the ground.

"Ow, that hurts! When my dad hears of this, we're going to sue you!"

"I don't think that will prevent you from going to jail on dealing and murder charges," Rogers said.

"Murder charges?" Brina asked as she continued to fight the handcuffs.

"We wondered who was wearing the red shirt when Leo was killed." Smythe held the photo toward her. "Looks like we know now."

Brina stopped struggling and the officers helped her to her feet. "That's ridiculous. I threw that shirt on because I wasn't quite dressed when Leo came to give me my orders for the night. As soon as we'd concluded our business, I went back to my room to get ready and tossed the shirt back in Claire's room. I was with Leo and I was wearing that shirt, but I didn't kill him."

I saw the thoughtfulness on the detective's face as she weighed the truth of what she was saying, so I crept to her shoe and tugged her pant leg. She looked down at me, up at the crowd, and back down again.

"So you were wearing the shirt but you ditched it before he died," she said, kneeling down and re-tying her shoelace.

"Swipe through the next photos," I whispered.

Nodding, she rose and looked through the phone again. She angled the display to Rogers, who raised her eyebrows and glanced at her partner before scanning the group. Curious, I stood on my hind feet and stretched tall. The detective rewarded me by slanting the phone where I could see it. Claire was in the photo, being pulled into the house by Leo. She was wearing the red shirt.

"Ms. Ormsby, maybe you'd like to come inside where we could have a private talk?" Rogers asked.

All eyes turned to Claire, who gazed at them wildly before exploding into tears.

"It was an accident!" she blubbered before descending into unintelligible sobbing.

Detective Rogers stepped to her side and cradled her gently, one arm around her shoulder and the other holding her hand. "Why don't we go inside and sit down?" she soothed. "You can take your time."

"I'm afraid we're going to have to keep your phone for evidence…Tyler, was it?" Detective Smythe held the phone up and waved it. "And you'll need to answer a couple of questions, too."

EIGHTEEN

LATER THAT NIGHT, Olivia and Ashley sat on the patio with glasses and a bottle between them. They had ditched the frivolity of margaritas and were now drinking straight tequila. Em and I wandered to the kitchen to find more food. Detective Smythe was still sitting at the table, pen in hand, leafing through a notepad.

There was a bowl of potato chips next to her, so I crawled up the table leg and helped myself to a wide, salty chip. It felt risky to sit and eat in front of a human, but I was hoping for a little courtesy after I helped her solve the case. Still, I sat facing her, ready to escape if she reached for me.

"Thank you, Hazel," she said, not looking up from her notes.

"Was it about the drugs?" I asked.

"Not really." She sighed. "Claire hadn't seen Brina wearing her shirt. When she came in from the shower to dress, she put it on and went outside—she was mending a tear in her shorts. Leo came out of his den so completely hammered, he saw the red shirt and thought she was Brina. Dragged her inside for some reason. She had the scissors in her hand, trying to get away from him, you can guess the rest." She looked over at me. "That is, I think you can guess. You are a mouse."

"Yes, Detective. It was an accident." I nibbled the edges of the chip, enjoying the saltiness.

"You know, you make a pretty good detective yourself," she said. "Course, I don't know where you'd carry a badge."

Mice don't laugh, but I made a kind of gurgling squeak that surprised even me. "I think it's time for me to go home. Detecting isn't really my favorite thing to do."

"What is your favorite thing?"

I wiggled my nose, thinking.

Em appeared beside me, holding a chip of his own. "Eating is my favorite."

"Eating's not bad," I said. "I think, if you'll excuse me, I'll get some sleep. Olivia is leaving tomorrow, and I don't want to miss my ride home." I turned to Em. "Are you coming with me?"

He chewed around the rim of the chip in his paws. "I'm not so sure anymore. I want to stay with you but when I think about leaving this place…does your house have an ocean?"

I shook my head. "I wish it did."

Back in Olivia's room, I crawled through the crack to the space my family had made home when I was born. My mother had lived here, nested here, planned to have us here, until she found herself at the pier and giving birth in the storm. Then the lightning came, and everything changed.

I curled into a ball and closed my eyes, feeling the house and the beach calling for me to stay. I also felt the melancholy of loss and wanted to leave. It was a restless night.

Olivia had told Ashley to be ready early the next morning, but I knew that Olivia's definition of early was slightly after noon, so I scampered down to the beach one last time at sunrise to feel the water wash over my toes and let them sink into the sand. Could I stay here forever with Em? He was a naïve little mouse and I enjoyed showing him how the world works. But I promised to return to my family.

I returned to the beach house to noise and humans. Olivia was on the patio having breakfast with a familiar face—her father. As I reached the steps, Ashley came to the table, along with an older man.

"I just don't understand why you didn't call me," Olivia's dad said. "If Ashley's father hadn't called me, I wouldn't have known all this was going on."

"I tried calling you, Daddy, but it went to voice-mail." Olivia stared at her coffee. "I decided I was an adult, I'd handle it all."

"I'm sorry, Sweetheart. I did get the first message and planned to call you back. I didn't think it was urgent, or I'd have called right away."

I sat and rubbed my whiskers, wondering if that was true.

"I just don't understand why you kept Leo on," she said. "Do you know he had cameras in all the rooms? Daddy, he was creepy."

"I'm sorry." Her father rubbed his forehead. "It's complicated. When I was young, I was sometimes impulsive and, well, a stupid young man. I got into some trouble—it doesn't matter what it was, but Leo helped cover it all up. I thought it was because we were friends. Turns out, it was his way of living off my payroll—he knew I was studying to be a doctor and that could mean a steady blackmail income for him."

Ashley looked up from her avocado toast. "I guess if you'd fired him, he'd still be alive."

"What a ghastly thought," Ashley's father said.

"But true." Olivia nodded. "At least, he wouldn't have died in our house." She took a long sip of coffee. "We have a murder house now."

I listened to their words, trying to find the morbidity in living here. It was now officially a "murder house." It was no use. I wouldn't describe my moral compass as being fine-tuned, but I couldn't see a reason to blame the house for Leo's murder. I felt a nudge at my shoulder, so I turned.

"Good morning, Em—" Except it wasn't him.

It was my dad.

"Dad!" I squeaked in proper mouse, as he did not speak English. "Why are you here? How?"

"I missed you, too." His squeak was probably still high for human ears, but it sounded old and gruff to me. "I hitched a ride with Mr. Bent this morning."

"But why?"

"Well, I heard Mr. Bent on the phone. I couldn't understand all the words, but I knew he was upset, and I got worried about you."

"Thanks, Dad, but I'm ok. I'll tell you all about it on our way home."

"Oh, that's the other thing," he squeaked. "I'm moving back here. Thought you'd want to stay anyway, and I'm ready to be back on the beach."

I jumped and squealed in my delight, coming down to nuzzle at my dad in pure bliss.

"What are you doing?" Em said as he climbed down from the roof.

Dad sat back, staring at the white mouse that spoke human. "Who's he?"

Turning to my dad, I said, "Dad, this is Em Ten Twelve, Em for short. He's a lab mouse who only ever learned to speak human." Then I turned to Em. "Em, this is my dad. He's come to live here again so I can stay, and we can all live at the beach."

It was Em's turn to jump with happiness, so he did.

"Can we go see the ocean now?" Dad asked.

I translated for Em and he said, "Oh, yes. You can let the water rush over you and let the sand suck you down."

"What did he say?" Dad asked.

"Don't mind him," I squeaked, and nudged Em forward. These two were going to have to learn each other's language.

In the meantime, we'd visit the waves together from now on.

ACKNOWLEDGMENTS

Well, I shall have to thank the two cohorts who talked me into writing this little cozy. Merrie Destefano and DeAnna Cameron (aka DeAnna Drake) approached me one Friday morning at the Corner Bakery during our monthly writers' lunch. When they gazed at me with puppy-dog eyes and asked if I'd write the third leg of this series, I said of course, thinking it would be a quick exercise in writing a cozy whodunit. Who knew it would end up being so hard, that I would become so invested in these little mice, that I'd write and rewrite until it was just right?

Who knew writing a story in first-person mouse could be so much fun?

I'd also like to thank my grandmother, Myrtle Gail Wetherholt for teaching me how to tell a story and giving me a love for animals, from the very large to the very small.

ABOUT THE AUTHOR

M.G. Wetherholt is a delicate lady of a certain age who delights in knitting, baking, digging for worms in the garden, and solving murders. When she's not at home, she's usually galloping a magnificent steed somewhere.

She is also an homage to my grandmother. Myrtle Gail Wetherholt could knit, crochet, and sew. Her pie crusts were to die for, and she could whip up a meal for a dozen people in an hour and keep everyone entertained while she did it. She loved the outdoors, planting unusual seeds in her garden to see how they grew (cotton, peanuts, etc), and yes, digging up worms to take fishing with her.

My most important memories with her are the evenings that she entertained company. I would sit on the carpet by her chair, and she would run her hands down my hair, giving my shoulders a rub here and there, and tell stories of her youth. It was here that I learned to be a storyteller.

She's been gone for 32 years now, and yet her wisdom and love and storytelling are still with me.

So you could say M.G. Wetherholt collaborated on this book with her granddaughter, Gayle Carline. And the only thing about our biography that isn't true is that neither of us is a delicate lady.

Enjoy,

Gayle Carline

You can find more about me at www.gaylecarline.com.

As Gayle Carline:

Freezer Burn (A Peri Minneopa Mystery)

Hit or Missus (A Peri Minneopa Mystery)

The Hot Mess (A Peri Minneopa Mystery)

A More Deadly Union (A Peri Minneopa Mystery)

Clean Sweep (A Peri Minneopa Short Story)

Murder on the Hoof

From the Horse's Mouth: One Lucky Memoir

What Would Erma Do? Confessions of a First Time Humor
Columnist

Are You There, Erma? It's Me Gayle

You're from Where?

Raising the Perfect Family and Other Tall Tales

Holly Jolly Holidays

As G.S. Carline:

Red Dragon Rising (Dragon Shadows Trilogy Book 1)

Moon Dragon Falling (Dragon Shadows Trilogy Book 2)

New Dragon Soaring (Dragon Shadows Trilogy Book 3)

HAVE YOU READ ALL THE BOOKS IN THIS SERIES?

LESSONS IN LATTE

BY MERRIE DESTEFANO

Melvin Mouse can talk and read minds, but he's also a magnet for trouble. So, it's no surprise when he accidentally agrees to help find his sworn enemy—a missing cat. He might not survive this adventure!

Merrie Destefano writes cozy mysteries that contain a dash of danger and a pinch of magic, all wrapped up in a heartwarming happy ending. For more information, visit www.MerrieDestefano.com.